Fair Stands the Wind

CATHERINE LODGE

Meryton Press

OYSTERVILLE, WA

FAIR STANDS THE WIND

ISBN: 978-1-68131-018-3

Cover design by Zorylee Diaz-Lupitou
Images: 123RF and public domain
Layout by Ellen Pickels

For SC Roberts, Sarah Pesce, and Zorylee Diaz-Lupitou
who helped me polish my rough diamond and, as ever, for
Marcelle Gibson, who first persuaded me I could write.

Thank you from the bottom of my heart, you bobby-dazzlers.

Chapter One

The assembly rooms at Meryton were hot, crowded, and consumed with curiosity. The local oracles had prophesied the attendance of their new neighbour and, unlike the oracles of old, had gone on to estimate his fortune, his height, and his single state in uncommon, if implausible, detail. All that remained was to view the gentleman and his party, the oracles having fallen into dispute as to their number and relationship to the main attraction of the evening.

The five Bennet sisters had been kept close to their mother all evening, for that worthy lady was intent upon throwing some one or other of them into the path of the newly arrived Mr. Bingley as soon as possible and before Lady Lucas got to him or, worse, Mrs. Goulding and her bony niece.

Elizabeth Bennet did her best to stifle a sigh. Her mother's careful arrangements—"Jane, you must sit on my right and, Lydia, you on my left since you are the most handsome of my girls"—had left her isolated between her sister Mary and a pillar. Since the former had brought one of her interminable conduct books, she was scarcely more company than the latter. Elizabeth exchanged looks of commiseration with her best friend, Charlotte Lucas, also seated firmly beside her own mama, and did her best to possess her soul in patience.

On the stage, the serpent player gave a preparatory honk, and the band swept raggedly into the third set of the evening. The dancers bowed, curtsied, and began the figure, Mr. Wright leading off with his left hand as usual and being put firmly back in place by his partner. Elizabeth counted the people present, counted the ladies, subtracted the one from the other to produce the number of gentlemen—which gave the number of women who would be without partners—counted the number of feathers in Lady Lucas's headdress, divided the number of feathers by the difference between the number of ladies and the number of gentlemen, and was faintly cheered when the result turned out to be a prime number. She sighed and was just about to commence an attempt to calculate the floor space of the ballroom, based on an estimated average length and breadth of the floorboards, when the main event of the evening finally occurred.

The doors opened, and the party from Netherfield swept in, led by an undeniably handsome, if somewhat overdressed, lady. The object of everyone's curiosity was a smiling, young gentleman of perhaps four-and-twenty, regrettably shorter than the first entrant, whom he introduced as his sister. Despite that, he was by no means ill looking and appeared good-humoured, which—as Mrs. Phillips remarked in a rather too penetrating whisper—was better than mere longshanks any day of the week.

This remark gained immediate and unfortunate point when the rest of the party entered: another lady and gentleman, who ignored each other so pointedly they had to be married, and a final gentleman. The latter was a very tall, dark-haired young man, somewhat older than Mr. Bingley, well dressed in a dark blue coat of austere cut, who had chosen to disfigure a particularly fine countenance with a pair of green-lensed spectacles. The buzz of speculation, which had begun to die down, rose again to renewed heights, a noise that did not go unnoticed by its object who became—although it scarcely seemed possible—even more upright and impassive.

Mr. Bingley was making introductions, and an immediate and rather ill-bred silence fell as everyone strained to hear. "… my sister Hurst and her husband and my particular friend Captain Darcy of the Royal Navy."

There was a moment's fascinated silence until, after a hurried wave from Sir William Lucas, the band was recalled to its duty, and the set began from the beginning. Under cover of the music, a search for some source of information on this newcomer began with little attempt at concealment.

To everyone's surprise, it was young Mr. Goulding who supplied the keenly felt deficit. Denied a long and deeply desired career at sea by his position as his father's heir and by his mother's completely erroneous conviction that he was "delicate," he had been forced to satisfy himself with newspaper accounts of the war at sea. As he said to his friend Robert Lucas, "That must be Darcy of the *Achilles*. You must have read about him! Took the French privateer *Liberté* off Ushant last year and intercepted a prime convoy the year before. Made over £30,000 in prize money alone. Was captain in that business in the Baltic—you must have read about it, Bob; it was in all the papers!"

This was better than even the most enthusiastic mama could have dreamed. A wealthy sea captain who must be single, for when would he have had time to marry? And visiting Netherfield too—what could be more convenient?

"He must be in want of a fine, healthy, and above all, young wife," said Mrs. Bennet with a particularly unpleasant look in the direction of Charlotte Lucas. "Lydia, sit up straight and pull your shoulders back," she added in what she incorrectly thought was a whisper.

Elizabeth sighed and did her best to hide behind her pillar. Every time she thought her mother could embarrass her no further, she was proved wrong. Elizabeth did her best to convey her apologies by a look, but Charlotte, with colour rather higher than usual, was ignoring her.

The set ended, and Mr. Bingley wasted no time in soliciting an introduction to Jane. Elizabeth thought that she was probably the only person in the room who could see just how nervous her sister was. Although Jane was used to the attention paid to her beauty, the outbreak of speculation and comment that followed the invitation was still discomposing. Captain Darcy danced with Miss Bingley and, as far as Elizabeth could see, they exchanged no more than a handful of words throughout the set.

The set ended. Mr. Bingley was introduced to Amelia Wallace, and Captain Darcy was bowing before Charlotte Lucas. Elizabeth looked down to hide her grin as Lady Lucas returned Mrs. Bennet's ill-natured expression. When she looked up again, she saw Charlotte was pink with pleasure, for at seven-and-twenty she had been forced to concede the floor to younger girls for the last two years. Elizabeth thought Charlotte appeared in particularly good looks. The gossip had reached positively frenzied proportions as Charlotte and her partner threaded through the measure, especially as they exchanged considerably more conversation than the captain had shared with his previous partner.

Elizabeth shifted on her cane-bottomed chair and wished the evening were over. The anxiety that she had striven hard to suppress all evening flooded back, and she clasped her hands in her lap and began to calculate how many seconds might pass before she could hope they would be going home.

"Lizzy, if you cannot sit still like a Christian, you can take Kitty and repair the flounce on her hem. That clumsy Harker boy trod on it." Gathering up a complaining Kitty, Elizabeth headed to a room at the rear where a servant waited with pins and thread for such emergencies. Together they patched up the errant hem, although the length of the tear meant it took them quite a quarter hour to repair it. Kitty was wild to return to the dancing, but Elizabeth lingered near the door for a breath of cool, fresh air.

The stars were out, and the full moon was visible over the market cross. She stepped out a little way for a proper view and was startled to see the unmistakeable figure of Captain Darcy being helped into what was presumably Mr. Bingley's carriage.

As she returned to the light and heat of the ballroom, she thought to herself how unmannerly it was to be overcome by drink so early in the evening.

Shaking her head, Elizabeth returned to the dancers. The previous set had finished, and the next was almost complete. Charlotte was now dancing with the senior Mr. Harker, her colour still high, obviously enjoying the unaccustomed attention. Jane was partnered with Richard Lucas—no prospects there; Lady Lucas would see to that if Sir William did not—and Kitty and Lydia were bouncing around with a couple of younger sons, hardly more than children themselves. Elizabeth hated having to think about her sisters' marital prospects in this manner; it was so sordid. If it were just a case of Jane and herself, she knew they would both rather scrimp and save on £50 a year each, but Mama and the younger girls—! She halted that line of thought with a firm stamp of a mental foot.

She composed her face, straightened her back, marched back into the ballroom—a determinedly pleasant expression on her face—and took up her seat next to Mary. The set ended, Mr. Bingley asked Jane to dance once more, and Elizabeth's heart sank. No doubt, in her mother's mind, matters were now completely settled, and they could all live happily ever after on Mr. Bingley's money. It was so difficult to know what to want. Did she hope that Mr. Bingley would fall desperately, and preferably quickly, in love with Jane so that they could all batten onto him like leeches, or did she hope that he would not, in which case they could all live in genteel—and doubtless improvident—poverty instead? It was all so unfair! Mr. Bingley seemed like a pleasant young man. Why could he not have met Jane when the matter was not so unhappily pressing? She thought of her poor father alone at home, and her eyes filled with tears. She realised she would have to move her chair behind the pillar before everyone noticed.

"Oh, Lizzy, whatever is wrong?" It was Charlotte, escaping both her partner and her mother. "I do hope Mr. Bennet is not worse?"

Elizabeth shook her head. "No, it is not that." She nodded towards Mr. Bingley and Jane as they crossed hands and led the set down the room. "A pleasant new neighbour has come into our circle, and we are obliged to see him as some sort of quarry whom we are duty-bound to pursue."

Charlotte laid a hand on hers. "I am very much afraid, my dear, that this is the lot of all women without fortune. Your situation is merely more urgent than most." They sat for a moment, watching the dancers. "And he does seem very taken with Jane."

"Dear Jane!" said Elizabeth. "Who could fail to be taken with her? It is merely a shame that she is obliged to tow the rest of us behind her." Then, changing the subject firmly, she asked, "I am afraid you must have had a very uncomfortable set. I saw your partner being helped into a carriage outside. Did he make himself unpleasant?"

"Captain Darcy?" Charlotte looked surprised. "Not at all. He was perfectly polite. He is not perhaps a practised dancer nor an easy conversationalist. I must admit I had the impression that he was conversing by a sort of rote, the size of the hall, the number of couples, the fine weather—you know the sort of thing—but it was all unexceptional. We parted quite amiably. Mr. Harker came and asked me to dance, so I did not see the captain leave. Perhaps he was unwell?"

"Perhaps," said Elizabeth dubiously and then winced as she heard Lydia screaming with laughter, apparently oblivious to the disapproving looks, notably from Miss Bingley and the rest of the party from Netherfield. Charlotte patted her hand, and they sat in companionable silence until the assembly was over.

Mr. Bingley and his party managed to get away early, and Elizabeth was heartily grateful. She had heard her mother plotting to waylay him and invite him and his party to dine, or something equally improper, before visits were exchanged. Kitty and Lydia made nuisances of themselves in the carriage as usual, complaining about the draft and squeeze. Poor Mary was sunk in what Elizabeth was coming to suspect was silent misery and as for Jane, Elizabeth could only imagine the weight of the expectations placed upon her. As Mrs. Bennet fretted, speculated, and triumphed over their neighbours, Elizabeth could see her eldest sister sinking further and further into her own unhappy thoughts.

Longbourn was warm and welcoming. Only Mr. Hill, the butler, and Sarah, Mrs. Bennet's maid, had waited up, which meant that her father must be asleep and comfortable. That at least was some relief to Elizabeth's anxiety, as were Mrs. Bennet's fierce orders to Kitty and Lydia to be quiet and be sure not to wake their poor papa. Obviously, Doctor Wallace's instructions had finally sunk in. Elizabeth wondered, not for the first time, what the doctor had really said in his last interview with her parents.

She undressed for bed in the room she had shared with Jane since they were both small, then burrowed beneath the blankets for the welcoming warmth left by the hot brick. Jane was still brushing her hair, the hundred measured strokes that had always seemed like a complete waste of time to Elizabeth.

"What was Mr. Bingley like, Jane?" She had to ask, and very probably, Jane would welcome a chance to talk.

"Very pleasant. He comes from somewhere in Yorkshire. He intends to spend his inheritance on an estate and has taken Netherfield on liking."

"Yes, but what was he like?"

Jane shrugged, a most un-Jane-like gesture. "He seemed amiable—willing to be pleased with his company. It is so difficult to converse properly whilst dancing, but I should not object to furthering our acquaintance, and he is hardly hideous." She laid down her hairbrush and came over to sit on Elizabeth's bed. "I have been thinking—perhaps you should consider going to Aunt and Uncle Gardiner instead of me. If I have indeed caught Mr. Bingley's attention, I had better stay here while you go and"—her lips twisted—"try your luck in London."

For a moment, Elizabeth thought her sister was about to cry, but as the thought formed, she saw Jane wrestle herself back into her usual composure. What was the use of crying? They had discussed their situation for many hours, but the facts remained unaltered. Mr. Bennet was seriously ill, his estate and income were entailed on a male cousin, and unless at least one of them married and married well, the rest of the family would be consigned to a life of near destitution. While Jane and Elizabeth might be able to obtain employment as governesses or companions, the youth and frankly poor education of their younger sisters would bar them from any such position. Mrs. Bennet was unlikely to be able to manage on her daughters' tiny inheritances and would be obliged to throw herself on the mercy of her brother, whose own growing family could not help but restrict whatever provision his undoubted generosity would oblige him to make.

With her accustomed efficiency, Jane twisted her hair into its usual night-time plait, blew out the candle, and climbed into bed. As she tried to sleep, Elizabeth thought that not the least evil of their position was the creation of this knowing, measured, *worldly* Jane.

Chapter Two

The next day, Mr. Bennet was rather better after his first good night's sleep in almost a week, the return of the brighter weather lifting his spirits as it normally did. Elizabeth brought him his morning coffee and read the newspapers to him until Mr. Lester, the new steward, arrived. After checking that her father was not too tired, Elizabeth allowed him in to her father's room to discuss a little estate business.

Although it felt disloyal, she had to admit that the estate was currently in a more prosperous condition under Mr. Lester's management than it had ever been under her father's less exacting regime. It was all the more unfair that this would probably accrue to the benefit of her father's heir rather than to his closer family. The sudden illness that had struck him down at such a comparatively young age had quickly proved how sadly improvident that regime had been. When the seriousness of his illness had first become apparent, her father had instituted a regimen of retrenchment and economy, but after many years of indulging his own whims and those of his wife, it had proved difficult to lay aside more than a few—a very few—hundred pounds.

However, the sun was out, the dull drizzle that had depressed everyone's spirits had lifted, and Elizabeth was determined to seize the opportunity for an hour's walking in the woods about her home. The autumn leaves had all fallen, and the paths were sadly muddy, but she knew the area so well that she could predict with some certainty those walks where the footing would be sound. So she headed for the higher ground, threading her way between a stand of gloomy pines.

From her vantage point high about Longbourn, she could look towards

Netherfield and indulge herself in a few moments of happy daydreaming. Perhaps Mr. Bingley would fall helplessly in love with Jane and all their troubles would be over. The rest of them could settle in a little house in the neighbourhood, and gradually they would all find respectable, prudent husbands—though she resolutely refused to imagine what such a man would want with Kitty or Lydia—and live happily, or at least contentedly, ever after.

Below in the water meadows, she could see a group of men on horseback approaching, the tall upright figure of Captain Darcy in front. He rode rather well for a sailor, but surely, two accompanying grooms was a little excessive. She remembered reading somewhere that a ship's captain was treated as an absolute monarch aboard his ship; obviously, the gentleman liked a certain state. The three horsemen galloped past, but while the two grooms touched their hats, the rider in front made no acknowledgement. Bolt upright, green spectacles flashing in the sunlight, he towered over her and was gone.

She dropped a mocking curtsey to his retreating back and continued her walk, the daydream dispelled by a sudden excess of reality. She set her mind to the more immediate problem: Mr. Bingley. He was by far the most promising candidate to present himself. How to contrive further meetings? Her poor father could not be expected to call, and since he was known to be unwell, it was doubtful the Netherfield party would call on him. Moreover, it was unlikely that the ladies at Netherfield would be eager to extend their acquaintance in the country, having appeared quite determinedly above their company.

Somehow, Elizabeth decided, she would have to contrive to call. If it had been a case of calling on any other neighbour, she would simply have walked. Lizzy Bennet's strange habit of perambulating about the countryside was too well known now to attract any attention locally. However, it would never do to appear eccentric or unmindful of the proprieties in such an important case, so she resolved to approach Mr. Lester for the loan of a pair of horses. Their carriage was old-fashioned but in good condition, and if she could but arrange to leave her mother behind, an afternoon call would be an excellent start to what, she hoped, would soon become a closer acquaintance.

Unfortunately, wishing for her mother's absence was much easier than securing it. Mrs. Bennet seized upon the idea of a call with all her usual intemperate enthusiasm. She would call with Jane, and Lydia could come too, "for we cannot as yet be sure that he has finally decided, and Lydia is such a lively young girl." Elizabeth and the other girls could go call upon their Aunt Phillips and gather the local news instead, "for your father is resting and must not be disturbed."

Mrs. Phillips was, as usual, pregnant with news, her maid Sukey being a particular friend of Mrs. Needham, the housekeeper at Netherfield. Mr. Bingley had bought supplies for at least another two months; his sisters were demanding, disobliging sorts of women; Mr. Hurst was drunk every night as soon as the ladies retired from dinner; and Captain Darcy's valet, Mr. Starkey, was a real live sailor with a wooden leg and a pigtail and everything.

If this were not enough excitement, Mr. Bingley himself arrived to visit Mr. Phillips, and he was brought in to take tea with the ladies. He proved himself just as pleasant and conversable as he had been the previous evening. The men were the pleasantest group of fellows he had ever met, the ladies the kindest and prettiest. He was devastated to learn he had missed Mrs. Bennet and would make sure his sisters returned the call as soon as ever they could so he could accompany them. So much good humour was not perhaps evidence of a penetrating intelligence, but there was no folly to weary or ill manners to disgust, and really, he would be the perfect match for Jane—or for Jane as she had been before they had all been obliged to learn the sterner truths of their situation. Elizabeth wondered whether the new Jane would find this unwearying good humour irksome but then chided herself. If any of them had nothing worse to worry about in a husband than that, they would be obliged to give thanks on their knees.

Mrs. Phillips's house was a general resort for the young people of the town for, as she herself expressed it, "I do so like to have a cheery group of people around me."

Elizabeth was exchanging pleasantries with young Mr. Catteral when Mr. Bingley came up to speak to them, asking about pleasant walks and rides in the area. "I am afraid neither of my sisters is a great one for spending time out of doors, but Darcy and I are hoping to ride out and see something of the countryside. I have been asking your uncle, Miss Bennet, about hiring a steward who knows the area to show me my business, for I know I shall have to get to know the land and the tenants too."

Seizing her opportunity with both hands, Elizabeth pretended to consider while Jack Catteral chattered away about coveys and good runs with the local hunt. When he had wound down, she said, "It is a pity my father has not been able to call at Netherfield. You have probably heard that he is rather unwell." Mr. Bingley bowed. "For he has a set of particularly fine maps of the area that he had made by a surveyor from Town, an old friend of my Uncle Gardiner, which I am sure you would find most helpful."

Mr. Bingley was all interest. "I would not disturb Mr. Bennet for the world, but if your mother would not mind receiving Darcy and me, a look at those maps would be most helpful."

"Captain Darcy?" Elizabeth was rather startled.

"Oh goodness me, yes, I am no hand at all with a map. But Darcy, well, Darcy reads 'em like I read a book. Told me once he did some surveying himself as a boy, naval surveying, rocks and shoals and such, but I dare say it is all the same sort of thing." He grinned unselfconsciously. "They tried to beat mensuration into me at school. No use at all. Gave up on me in the end. So, Miss Bennet, if Darcy is well enough, poor fellow, I shall do myself the honour of calling at Longbourn tomorrow." With that, he bowed to the company and took his leave of Mrs. Phillips.

As Elizabeth watched him go, she wondered whether Captain Darcy was often unwell. Old Mr. Catteral was often "unwell" too, and she wondered whether it were the same malady: too much Port. Then suddenly she realised just how very uncharitable she was being. The poor man had served his country with distinction and no doubt hoped to do so again. A wound or illness contracted at sea was far more likely to be the cause of his absence. It would not do; it really would not do. She was allowing her own situation to cloud her judgement of her fellow man. Merely because people in Meryton were beginning to fight shy of their acquaintance—for fear of appeals for assistance when the worst occurred—was no excuse for ascribing the worst of motives and reasons to other people's actions, and to a stranger's at that.

The luck of the meeting with Mr. Bingley was all that made the evening supportable. Mrs. Bennet was bemoaning her misfortune at having missed him and complaining that Jane had wasted her blue muslin on his sisters, grand ladies who gave themselves airs for all the world as though their grandfather had not been a weaver and their father a dealer in wool and worsted. "Though that is the way of the world, and very unchristian it is too, I'm sure," said Mrs. Bennet, "for my girls are much better born, and yet they do not have £20,000 apiece." She fell to speculating what they would do if they had, a train of thought that Elizabeth believed would soon reveal how quickly that sum would be spent. "And as for that Captain Darcy! We saw him being carried upstairs to his room by his grooms just like Mr. Catteral, and it not three-thirty in the afternoon. Though it is all the same with these sailors, drinking and"—she remembered to whom she was talking and ended with a rather weak—"and such like."

The news that Mr. Bingley was probably to visit on the morrow sent her into fits of nerves and a flurry of orders. "Hill! Hill! We must be sure the library is swept and dusted, and Mr. Hill must go into town and fetch some of the good coffee. Jane, you must wear your blue muslin again, for it is particularly becoming, and his sisters will not be here to know you have worn it before."

When Mr. Bingley, accompanied by Captain Darcy, rode up the following day, the Bennet ladies were all in the large parlour, ostentatiously engaged in suitable womanly pursuits: sewing, netting, drawing, and such while listening to Mary read from *Fordyce's Sermons*, activities they were all only too glad to lay aside to greet the visitors.

Civil enquiries were exchanged about Mr. Bennet's health. Mr. Bingley was effusive but not ridiculously so, and Captain Darcy contented himself with a bow and a brief wish for Mr. Bennet's better health. It was not that he was curt, nor that he was haughty or ill mannered, more that he seemed ill at ease. Coffee was drunk and conversation had, mostly carried on by Mr. Bingley and Mrs. Bennet with occasional interjections from Jane, the younger girls having been firmly warned against interrupting any conversation Mr. Bingley might have with their eldest sister.

Eventually, the inspection of the maps could be postponed no longer. The library was too small to admit more than a few people, and since Jane and Mr. Bingley must be kept together, Elizabeth had been previously detailed to accompany her sister and the gentlemen, largely because Mrs. Bennet was obliged to admit that Elizabeth was the only one who would understand them. "And do not go showing away and making Mr. Bingley look foolish, for there is nothing gentlemen dislike more than clever women."

Mr. Hill unrolled the maps on the library table, and they leaned over to inspect them. With a muttered apology, Captain Darcy turned them until they were aligned north to south and then addressed himself to Mr. Bingley, pointing out where various landmarks lay in relation to Netherfield. Jane did her best to be interested and conversational, pointing out the bluebell dell and the parts of the river where the best fishing was to be had. "For my father particularly asked me to invite you to fish there if you are of a mind."

Captain Darcy, however, was staring at the map, his expression faintly dubious. Eventually he tapped one corner and asked, "Are you quite sure about this section here? For I rode down there yesterday, and the stand of trees and the hill were not quite as they are shown here."

This was something Elizabeth could answer, and even her mother could not object. "You are quite right, Captain," she said. "There was a small landslip during heavy rains in the year eight. Several fine trees and part of the hill had to be carted away to keep the road to Hatfield open. I have often wished I could amend the map, but alas, without the correct measurements, I have no doubt but that I should make the error worse. My father only keeps an eleven-yard chain, and I have never been able to find a trustworthy confederate who is prepared to stand around in the mud and help me with it." She looked up laughingly to see the captain's expression change from one of intelligent interest to something she could not identify: disapproval perhaps, or even ennui, for he no longer met her gaze and seemed more interested in the wallpaper. She shrugged mentally and was about to address a remark to Mr. Bingley when the captain spoke, his voice peremptory. "Come, Bingley, we have trespassed upon the ladies' hospitality long enough. It is time we were leaving."

Jane and Elizabeth protested, but Mr. Bingley turned to go obediently. As they walked into the hall, they heard running feet and turned to see the housekeeper. "Oh, Miss Bennet, Miss Elizabeth, your mother says you must come at once. Mr. Bennet has taken a turn."

It was not the worst, but it so easily could have been. The heartbreaking cough that convulsed his entire frame seemed to take an age to respond to Doctor Wallace's medicine, and it was very late before Mr. Bennet sank into an uneasy doze.

The whole house slept uneasily that night, and the next day Mr. Bennet sent for Elizabeth. He was sitting up on his usual chaise longue, his legs covered with a blanket. As she bent over to kiss his forehead, she noticed a letter in his hand.

After the usual enquiries and the usual falsely cheerful response, he handed her the letter. "I wrote to my heir, Mr. Collins, last week," he said.

"This is his reply."

It was a strange letter and one that left Elizabeth feeling more than somewhat uneasy. "What can he mean by apologising for the entail?" she said. "And what is this about making amends?"

Mr. Bennet stifled another cough. "He is not, it seems, a sensible man. However, I believe he may be coming here, at least in part, to seek a wife from amongst my daughters." He laid a hand on hers. "I deeply regret this, dearest, but unless he is the merest brute, it might well be for the best if one of you were to accept him."

"Oh, sir, surely it cannot be so very urgent?"

Her father shook his head. "Who can say? I may have months before me or merely days. However, as I have criminally done so little to provide for your mother and sisters, it seems that the burden will fall upon you." He sighed, which set him coughing again, and it was not until he had control of his breathing once more that he continued, "We both know that the younger girls will not do, and Jane has not the strength of mind to manage a foolish husband. It is not what I wanted for you, dear girl, and I know you will find it almost intolerably difficult to do, but unless some other prospect for you or Jane arises, I do not see that there is any choice—not if I am to leave you all without fearing for your very existence." He dropped his gaze but not before Elizabeth saw the tears in his eyes. "I am so very sorry, Lizzy. You all, but you and Jane in particular, deserve better."

Elizabeth took one of his hands in hers. How pale and thin it had become! "Do not be afraid. If I can provide for my mother and sisters by marrying this man, I shall. Who knows, he may be better than his letter promises. He would not be the first gentleman who failed to make the best of himself in correspondence." Mr. Bennet could not speak and had to content himself with patting her hand gently. She sat with him until he fell asleep.

There was no point in mentioning any of this to her mother or sisters, not until it should prove absolutely necessary. In the meantime, there was the annual invitation to dinner to celebrate the anniversary of Mr. and Mrs. Goulding's marriage, and since Mr. Bingley and his party were expected to be there, it was vital that Jane appear her best. Having "used up" the blue muslin, she must bring out the pink silk their Aunt Gardiner had sent from London, saved for just such a formal occasion and extremely becoming.

However, even the simple business of obtaining new ribbons to set off the dress and Jane to perfection brought an unwelcome reminder of their situation. Mrs. Finch the dressmaker hummed and hawed but ended by asking to be paid in cash rather than sending in her bill at the end of the month. Lydia was shrilly indignant as the sisters rummaged through their reticules for pennies and sixpences, but Elizabeth was more sympathetic, realising the woman was afraid that, if Mr. Bennet died, outstanding accounts would be delayed or perhaps not paid at all—a major blow to a widow in such a small way of business.

Luckily, Lydia and Kitty were swept up into preparations the moment they returned to Longbourn, and Elizabeth had the melancholy satisfaction of hiding from Jane that she had spent the last of her own pin money buying the ribbons. They had both been trying to exercise the strictest economy, but even so, both had managed to save little more than half the cost of the mourning clothes they might be obliged to wear all too soon.

Dinner at the Gouldings' the following day served to brighten all their spirits. Jane looked beautiful, and Mr. Bingley was obviously, but never offensively, attentive. Miss Bingley and the Hursts also came and distinguished themselves by ill manners, haughtiness and, in Mr. Hurst's case, excessive attention to Mr. Goulding's excellent Port.

Elizabeth found herself beside Miss Bingley after the ladies retired and, for want of any suitable subject of conversation, asked after the whereabouts of Captain Darcy, who was absent although she knew he had been invited.

Miss Bingley coloured, looked conscious, and then said, "He is visiting his brother in Derbyshire. The captain is one of the Darcys of Pemberley in Derbyshire, you know."

Having no idea what this portentous announcement signified, Elizabeth merely bowed and started a conversation on the state of the roads, the number of footpads said to be abroad, and the weather. Miss Bingley seemed disinclined to bear her share of the conversation and eventually drifted off to speak to her sister.

Left at a loose end, Elizabeth wandered into Mr. Goulding's library, where she knew there would be a county gazetteer, and looked up Pemberley. To her surprise, she found it was close to the small town of Lambton, where her Aunt Gardiner had spent much of her early life. She read the details of the impressive house and estate. The current owner, George Arthur Darcy, must be the brother Miss Bingley had mentioned.

She heard the unmistakeable sound of Mary playing the piano in the drawing room and returned to find the company joined in an energetic jig. Young Mr. Goulding had obviously forestalled any other invitation for Jane, for the two of them were now crossing hands at the top of the set. Mrs. Bennet was scowling in a corner but Elizabeth fancied it would do no harm for Mr. Bingley to realise he was not the only gentleman with eyes for Jane.

As she sat beside her mother, Elizabeth found her thoughts turning to her father's heir, Mr. Collins. His letter had been notably ill-written, combining sycophancy with an imperfectly hidden and most improper eagerness to take up possession. Mrs. Bennet was complaining about something, but Elizabeth could hardly hear her, her mind insisting upon repeating some of the more infelicitous phrases from Mr. Collins's letter over and over again. This was the man her father thought she must marry, and what little she knew of him was no inducement to respect—still less to the more tender feelings she had always hoped to offer her husband.

Chapter Three

I f the Gouldings' dinner had not settled the matter to Mrs. Bennet's satisfaction, a letter came three days later that quickly convinced her that their troubles were over. Miss Bingley wrote to invite Jane for luncheon and tea. Contriving to the height of her powers, Mrs. Bennet arranged for Jane to go on horseback, confident that the weather would break and strand her daughter in the same house as Mr. Bingley.

Sure enough, Jane had been gone less than an hour when the heavens opened in a brief but drenching rain shower. Some time later, a letter was brought announcing that Jane had been caught in it and was now unwell. "People do not die of trifling colds," said Mrs. Bennet confidently, only to recollect and add, "Young people, at any rate." She called for the housekeeper. "Hill! Hill! We must send over Miss Elizabeth's new nightgown and slippers, for they are much nicer than Miss Jane's, and it would not do for the house to think us all paupers." She paused as though waiting for Elizabeth to object to this summary appropriation of her birthday present, but when no objection came, she continued to Elizabeth's horror, "Perhaps, Mr. Bingley will visit her—now, it is no use you looking like that, Lizzy. You do not know what gentlemen are, and if he can only be induced to compromise her, we shall all be safe."

This was quite enough to decide Elizabeth that she must visit Jane as soon as possible. The very next day she set off across the fields and lanes, clambering over stiles and leaping over puddles, determined to arrive as soon as possible, no matter the jeopardy to her shoes and stockings.

There was no doubt that Miss Bingley and Mrs. Hurst were, or pretended to be, much shocked at her arrival in this manner. However, Mr. Bingley was all that was welcoming and quickly ordered a maid to take her up to Jane's room. It was soon evident that Jane was really unwell, and with her father's health so much in the foremost of her mind, Elizabeth was happy to agree to Mr. Bingley's suggestion that the apothecary be sent for.

Jane grew more feverish and uncomfortable as the hours passed, and it was only when Mr. Johns arrived and reassured them all that it was merely a bad cold that Elizabeth felt she could leave her sister. It was by then too late for her to return to Longbourn, so she readily accepted the invitation to dine and stay the night.

It was obvious that Mr. Bingley was truly concerned and that Miss Bingley and Mrs. Hurst merely pretended to be. When Elizabeth eventually left Jane to go and dine, she overheard those ladies engaged in abusing their acquaintance. When they had exhausted that entertainment, they both moved to wondering what could have kept Captain Darcy, who had been expected back that day, and wishing he were there already. Remembering the gazetteer, Elizabeth realised that, for a lady in Miss Bingley's position, Captain Darcy, a wealthy member of a much-lauded profession with an independent fortune and aristocratic connections, was a prize well worth bestowing her £20,000 on.

She wondered whether the captain had any views on the subject, or even whether he was to be allowed any. Miss Bingley would doubtless scorn Mrs. Bennet for her matchmaking, but in ambition and cast of mind, there was little to choose between them.

After a dull evening in which only Elizabeth seemed to be content to sit with a book, which she soon discovered held the missing gentleman's bookplate, they all retired for the night. Jane was asleep when she checked; so, unwilling to disturb her, Elizabeth went to her own room.

Elizabeth had been given the room next to Jane's and left the doors to both rooms open in case Jane needed her during the night. A little after midnight, she was awakened by the sounds of a carriage outside and voices and running feet in the hall below. The same noises had obviously awakened Jane, for Elizabeth heard her name being called.

Swiftly, she wrapped a shawl about her shoulders and tiptoed to the door of her room. She could see the light of candles in the hall and hesitated in case someone should come upstairs.

The voice of Captain Darcy rang clearly up the stairs. "I am so very sorry, Bingley, but I could think of nowhere else to go. If we can but rest here for a few days, I shall arrange to rent a place I can take them to."

Mr. Bingley replied with all the gruffness of an English gentleman caught in the act of being generous, "Think nothing of it, my dear fellow. Mrs. Needham is making up the rooms now. Come into the library; there is a fire in there, and tea will be along in two shakes."

As Elizabeth scurried into Jane's room, she heard Mr. Bingley exclaim, "Oh, what a truly damnable business!"

Jane had an uncomfortable night and did not truly fall asleep until almost dawn. As Elizabeth left her sister, she could hear the house beginning to stir. Despite her restless night, she was determined to come down for breakfast, for it would never do to give the impression that the Bennets were lie-a-beds.

She need not have worried as only the gentlemen were present when she arrived. Mr. Bingley was quick to enquire after her sister, and even Captain Darcy managed a few civil words. He seemed unaffected by a disturbed night, and Elizabeth reflected that a captain at sea must be accustomed to a lack of rest.

She had almost finished her repast when Miss Bingley swept in, bearing the unmistakeably signs of someone not used to early mornings and doing her best to hide the fact. Watching her greet her brother, and especially the captain, Elizabeth realised that Miss Bingley knew someone had arrived in the night but had not yet been informed who it was, and she was consumed by a curiosity it would have been most ill bred to display. She had just begun with, "Charles, I understand—" when there was an almighty crash of broken china from somewhere close that quite drowned what she was about to say.

In the dead silence that followed the crash, Elizabeth heard the sound of running feet and a boy crying out, "I am sorry, Mrs. Needham—I am, I am; it just sort of slipped." She could not hear the reply, and the voices disappeared downstairs as someone came to sweep up the broken pieces.

"Really, Charles! How many times have I told you? We have to get rid of the boy before he breaks every piece of china we have!"

Mr. Bingley looked self-conscious. "Caroline, I told you. I promised Reverend Carter to find a place for the boy so he would not have to go on the parish, poor lad, and he is perfectly willing—just clumsy." He turned to Elizabeth. "I appeal to you, Miss Bennet: What would you do?"

Elizabeth hesitated, unwilling to interfere with another woman's house-keeping, but the look of indignation on Miss Bingley's face spurred her to reply. "Well, if it were up to me, I would put the boy to work in the stables. Is it the youngest Dalton, by the way? I know there were five children to place when the parents died. If it is, Mr. Dalton was our local farrier, so the boy is used to horses. If you still need someone in the house, Mrs. Needham is a local woman. She is sure to know of a lad who would suit."

Mr. Bingley sat back in his chair and blew out his cheeks with relief. "Bravo, Miss Elizabeth. All our problems solved in one go. A Solomon come to judgement indeed."

Miss Bingley appeared about to expostulate when a maid entered, curtsied to the captain, and said, "Excuse me, sir, but the young lady was asking after you." The gentleman quickly rose, tossed his napkin on the table, and with a bow to the ladies, left the room. After a few seconds, Elizabeth followed suit, realising that Miss Bingley was about to start an argument with her brother that she had no wish to witness.

Upstairs, she found Jane still asleep, so she left her to return to her own room. However, as she stepped into the corridor, she discovered Captain Darcy waiting for her. He bowed, appeared uncomfortable, and then said, "If you have a moment, Miss Bennet, may I ask for your assistance with my sister?" He looked at the carpet, at the wallpaper, and then at Elizabeth. He was not wearing the green spectacles, and for the first time, she saw that his eyes were an attractive deep brown. "I brought my sister and her mother with me last night. My sister is unwell but is understandably unwilling to discuss what is wrong with an elder brother she has not seen for over five years. I would ask Mrs. Darcy, but she had a very disturbed night and is still sleeping." For the first time, he looked tired but ploughed on. "Am I asking too much if I request you to see whether there is anything to be done? She is very shy, but since you have younger sisters, I feel sure you are the best person in the house to help. I shall, of course, wake her mother if need be, but I would prefer not to if it can be avoided."

Elizabeth professed her complete willingness and waited while he knocked on his sister's door. "May I come in, sweetheart?" he said gently. Captain Darcy must have taken the confused murmur from inside as assent because he waved Elizabeth to enter with him.

There was a maid was in the room and a fair young lady in the bed. At first

Elizabeth took her for perhaps seventeen or eighteen years of age but soon realised that she was rather younger, for all her womanly form and features.

"Dear, this is Miss Elizabeth Bennet," he said. "She is staying at Netherfield with her sister, and I thought it might be easier for you to talk to her than your old sea-dog of a brother. Miss Bennet, my sister Georgiana." Elizabeth curtsied and did her best to appear all that was amiable and helpful. "I shall be off now, but if you need me at all, you know you must send for me immediately."

The pale face in the bed smiled and said timidly, "Aye, aye, Captain." Elizabeth watched as Captain Darcy's lips compressed and he looked away, obviously deeply affected, then he strode over to the bed, kissed his sister on the forehead, and left the room.

Left alone, Elizabeth went over to the bed. With a smile and a "do you mind?" she sat on the counterpane and took the young lady's hand in hers. "Now, what is it I can do to help, my dear?" she said.

It took a great deal of blushing and stammering before Elizabeth gathered that it was nothing more than a case of a very shy young lady in a strange house with very little baggage, who had been surprised by the early arrival of her courses before she had made provision for the usual rags. Turning to the maid, Elizabeth dealt with the immediate problem, ordered a little breakfast for Miss Darcy, and set her mind to putting that young lady at something approaching her ease.

She quickly realised that Miss Darcy, or Georgiana as she was soon invited to call her, was for some reason unwilling to talk about her home or the reason for the visit on which she had just embarked. However, she was more than happy to talk about the brother who had just left, even if she would not talk about the one she had left behind in Derbyshire.

As far as Georgiana was concerned, Captain Darcy was all that was kind and generous. "For we had a post-chaise all the way and stopped three times at various inns. He would not let us pay for anything even though I had my pin money and Mama had several guineas in her purse. Maids to see to us, the best of everything—he even got me a new"—here she blushed—"nightgown when my old one fell out of my bag while it was being loaded at Stamford."

Elizabeth was beginning to wonder whether she should be hearing these artless confessions. It was surely very odd that a young lady from such a wealthy family should be so unused to those attentions that even families like her Uncle Gardiner's expected as no more than their due whenever they travelled.

The breakfast arrived, and Elizabeth took the chance to leave and reassure the captain, whom she found loitering in the hallway for her. In a few brief words, she did her best to make such explanations as she thought fit for him to hear and was pleased by his evident comprehension and gratitude. She was about to return upstairs to see how Jane was faring when she saw him sway suddenly on his feet. He was far too tall for Elizabeth to think of supporting him, and there was no one on duty in the hall, so she seized a chair from against the wall and dragged it over so that he could sit or, rather, collapse into it.

She was just about to ring for a footman when the captain raised his voice in a bellow that, she reflected, must have been trained by many a storm at sea. "Starkey!"

After a few seconds, she heard the sound of pounding feet, and the famous valet appeared, local report having once more lied, for in the matter of legs he had an undeniably complete set. He was also dressed in the decent sub-fusc of an upper servant, even if he did have an impressive pigtail hanging halfway down his back.

"You'm not been wearing your giglamps," he scolded, producing the spectacles from a pocket. "You know what Mr. Luscombe said."

"Luscombe's an old woman, and you are another." However, the captain took the spectacles and put them on. "I do not think they make a damned bit of difference." He squeezed his eyes shut and lay back in the chair. "Is Miss Bennet still there?"

"Yes, sir," she replied.

"Pray, accept my apologies for the language. I am afraid I am not bearing my troubles with equanimity. Would you be so very kind as to keep an eye open for my sister and Mrs. Darcy? I shall have to go and lie down for a while."

Elizabeth assured him of her willingness to do so, reproaching herself silently for her earlier lack of charity. The poor man was obviously wounded or unwell.

"Is Anderssen there?" he asked as another man, this one in the sailor's traditional blue jacket and wide trousers, came thundering down the stairs.

"Aye, sir."

"Then help me upstairs. Miss Bennet, your servant."

Foolishly, Elizabeth curtsied although his eyes were still shut, and the two seamen half-led, half-carried him upstairs.

Jane was awake and dressing when Elizabeth next called in to see her. It was almost time for luncheon, and Jane was feeling so much better that it was decided that they would go down together once Elizabeth had called on the other ladies.

Georgiana was still in bed and confessed, on close but kindly questioning, that she was in some discomfort. So Elizabeth ordered a small stone bottle filled with hot water and wrapped in flannel to ease her pain. Once again, the poor young lady seemed bemused by such kindness but still managed to say all that was grateful.

However, when Elizabeth knocked on the door next to Georgiana's, a maid answered that Mrs. Darcy had eaten but was still very tired and preferred not to see anybody at the moment. "And," said the maid, whom Elizabeth recognised as a cousin of their Hill, "if I let you in, I'd 'ave to let that Miss Bingley in too, and she's already sent her maid round with 'er ears 'anging out. The poor lady don't need botherin' no more and that's a fact." Then, obviously realising that she had said more than it was her place to, she scurried back into the bedroom.

Elizabeth shared something of all this with Jane before they went down-stairs, and Jane agreed that it would be kind to visit Miss Darcy after they had eaten. She also suggested that reading to her might help to take her mind off her aches and pains.

They had just reached the head of the main staircase down to the hall when they heard an all-too-familiar voice. "Oh, Mr. Bingley, I am sure you have been all that is generous, but a mother's anxiety, sir, you can have no idea of. With my poor dear Bennet so very ill, I felt I just had to come and see how poor Jane is doing. I am sure you will remember my youngest daughter, Lydia."

Lydia giggled. "Oh, Ma," she said, "how you do go on!"

Chapter Four

Swiftly, Elizabeth grasped her sister's arm and dragged her out of sight. Jane would have protested, but Elizabeth succeeded in motioning her into silence and back into her bedroom.

"Elizabeth, that was Mama. We must go down and see her."

"No, we must not," said Elizabeth, searching for her sister's nightgown. "You must get back into bed immediately. You know you are here entirely by Mama's contrivance. What do you think she will say if she sees that you are recovered and ready to return home? Can you not imagine how indignant she will be to find all her plots and plans so thoroughly undermined?" She did not mention how that indignation would be expressed; she did not have to, for Jane began to undress hurriedly, urging Elizabeth to help her with buttons and ties.

She was under the sheets just in time, for a knock came at the door shortly after, a maid sent to enquire whether Miss Bennet was ready to receive her mother. Jane squeezed her eyes shut as Elizabeth opened the door a crack and whispered that her sister had just that minute closed her eyes and that she, Elizabeth, would come down.

When she arrived downstairs, she found her mother and Lydia ensconced in the drawing room, drinking tea and talking with all their usual thoughtless inanity. Mrs. Bennet was extolling Jane's virtues to a fascinated Mr. Bingley and a highly suspicious Miss Bingley and Mrs. Hurst. "I have no idea what could have happened to Jane, for she has not had a day's illness since she was very small. Such a healthy young girl, and as for her temperament, you could not wish for a sweeter—no, nor a kinder—and although I say it—who should not—she is a girl in whom beauty of face is just a sign of the greater beauty within."

Meanwhile, Lydia was attempting to persuade Mr. Bingley to hold a ball. "... for with the militia newly arrived in the village, there shall be partners for all, and I shall not have to stand up with Mr. Wright who does not know his 'Sir Roger de Coverley' from his 'Gathering Peascods,' and even if he did, he does not have a red coat and a sword."

When Elizabeth entered, she was assailed with enquiries from Mrs. Bennet about Jane's health, and she knew she was not the only person in the room to read her mother's determination that Jane stay exactly where she was for the time being. Mrs. Bennet's elephantine ideas of sophistication were transparent to anyone of ordinary intelligence. Luckily, Mr. Bingley seemed too interested in and concerned for Jane to have noticed.

Once Mrs. Bennet had assured herself that her plans were—as she considered it—working to perfection, she attempted to gather up Lydia and depart. Lydia, however, had not given up her attack upon their host and his hospitality, which gave Elizabeth a chance to enquire after her father.

In the background, Lydia finally received the promise she had been begging for, but it meant little compared to Mrs. Bennet's news. She took Elizabeth's arm and turned her away from the party. "He is no worse, Lizzy, but I cannot say he is any better. That horrid cough—and he does not seem to sleep. And now that dreadful Mr. Collins is coming to inspect Longbourn and work out how soon he can put us all out into the hedgerows, and what I shall do without Mr. Bennet, I do not know." For the first time ever, Elizabeth could see what her mother would look like as an old woman; her exasperation drained away, and she helped Mrs. Bennet into the family coach with more tenderness than—her conscience reproached her—she had shown for some time.

The day was fine, and after she had waved the coach away, she took a turn about the gardens. She could see where the neglect of several years was being repaired and found a warm, sunny terrace where she could sit and consider her situation.

Neither she nor Jane could stay for more than another night. Quite apart from the encroachment on Mr. Bingley's hospitality, she was wild to be home to see how her father did. Tomorrow, yes—she would request the loan of a coach tomorrow, and they would both return, even if, as seemed likely, nothing was settled between Jane and Mr. Bingley. Indeed, while Jane kept to her bed, nothing could be settled. Well, at least when they returned home they would face Mrs. Bennet's objections in decent privacy.

Having thus determined her course of action, she set off back into the house. As she passed through the hallway on her way to see Jane and Miss Darcy, she heard Miss Bingley's voice raised in complaint. "Charles, you cannot possibly mean to gratify that dreadful chit and hold a ball here in these savage backwoods."

"Yes, I do, Caroline. It is time we took up our position in the society of the neighbourhood." Elizabeth could hear him shaking out a newspaper, the gentleman's ever-ready resource in times of domestic dispute.

Miss Bingley was not that easily out-manoeuvred. "But I am sure the poor, dear captain is far too ill to be disturbed by the *society* afforded by country neighbours."

Mr. Bingley, like many good-natured men before him, had been pushed too far, and he had obviously decided to make a stand. "My dear Caroline, Darcy has seen considerably coarser society than he will see at our ball, and if he overtires himself again, he may retire and lie down until he feels better."

"But—"

"Next full moon should give us ample opportunity to make preparations and send out invitations. May I leave that to you? Or shall I leave it all to Mrs. Needham?"

As she climbed the stairs towards the bedchambers, Elizabeth wondered whether that last comment had been innocently made or whether Mr. Bingley had unsuspected Machiavellian depths.

That night, both Miss Darcy and the hitherto-unseen Mrs. Darcy came down to dinner, arriving a little after Elizabeth and Jane. Mrs. Darcy was a small, colourless woman, rather younger than she had expected; indeed, she seemed little older than the stepson on whose arm she entered. Both ladies were dressed simply, and Miss Darcy's gown had quite obviously been darned. From their expressions, the sight did not escape either Miss Bingley or Mrs. Hurst, although both ladies exerted themselves to be charming and hospitable.

Neither mother nor daughter contributed much to the conversation at table. Miss Darcy was quite obviously shy, and Miss Bingley was soon using her for a sort of conversational target practice, directing a stream of bright, false chatter in the young lady's general direction without waiting for any response. Mr. Bingley attempted to speak to Mrs. Darcy but soon retired, defeated in the face of a thin trickle of "Yes, sirs" and "No, sirs," and it was left to Jane to do her best to entertain and put the older lady at her ease.

The captain, in response to Elizabeth's question, professed himself quite recovered and spent the meal staring worriedly at his sister and her mother. In an effort to enliven the evening, Elizabeth thought to ask Mr. Bingley how he and the captain had come to be friends.

Mr. Bingley seized on the topic at once. "We met in France," he said, adding hurriedly, "in the Peace, of course. My father sent me over as soon as the treaty was signed. I think he hoped I would acquire a little Town bronze. I met Darcy a few miles outside Calais when Boney broke the peace and started detaining travellers. I did not much care for the idea of the fortress at La Bîche; the rumour was it was most unpleasant. Captain Darcy and I were in the same hotel and both decided to skip the place and try for the coast." He smiled gaily. "Dashed horrible it was too. Took us a week to sneak through France, raining all the way, and then we had to wait 'til Darcy found us a fishing boat he could sail to England."

"You make it sound much more exciting that it was," interrupted the captain. "We were not twenty miles from the coast, and I had every confidence we would meet the Channel Fleet—and we did, less than five miles from shore. And once we did, we were home and dry."

"Not exactly dry," protested Mr. Bingley, and went on to describe the hardships of life in a war sloop of His Majesty's Royal Navy. "While the hanging cots are very comfortable, I regret I never got used to the way the walls kept opening up and squirting me with ice-cold seawater." This at least had the effect of distracting Miss Bingley from her pursuit of Miss Darcy, and the rest of the dinner passed in her commiserations to the captain for the rigours of his life afloat and his attempts to assure her that, as captain of a ship of the line, it had been many years since he had slept in a shower-bath.

When the ladies retired, with Mr. Bingley's pledge that the gentlemen would not be long, Miss Bingley seemed ready to recommence her assault of Georgiana. Elizabeth, however, was prepared. She affected to see signs of fatigue, where in truth there was only shyness and discomfort, and suggested that Mrs. Darcy and her daughter retire. The eagerness with which Miss

Darcy seized on the proposal soon persuaded Elizabeth that she had been right to act. The two Darcy ladies retired, and Elizabeth and Jane went up with the younger lady to see she had everything she needed.

Once Georgiana was settled for the night and a maid was seeing to Mrs. Darcy, Jane, too, retired, exhausted by the evening after her recent illness. Elizabeth, however, went downstairs, resolving to request the carriage for the morrow.

As she crossed the hall, she could hear the querulous tones of Miss Bingley, no doubt complaining about the escape of her prey. Refusing to be daunted and quite out of patience with that lady, Elizabeth sailed into the drawing room, head held high, and had the satisfaction of reducing her hostess to red-faced silence.

Captain Darcy brought her a cup of coffee and sat beside her. "Is my sister quite well?" he asked.

"Just a little tired."

At the other end of the room, Miss Bingley was engaged in a furious whispered conversation with her sister while they searched through the available sheet music.

"You and Miss Bennet have both been very kind. I wonder whether I might trespass further on your good nature."

Elizabeth nodded.

"You have seen the state of my sister's clothing. Would it be possible for you to accompany her to Hatfield or some other local town and help her repair the deficiencies in her wardrobe? I fear she needs almost everything—a full rig. I shall of course repay your father, perhaps when the bills are submitted?"

Elizabeth smiled sadly. "Sir, you are inviting a lady to go shopping with someone else's money, and under normal circumstances I would be happy to oblige. However"—here she blushed and lowered her voice—"my father's illness has led to at least one of the local tradespeople withdrawing credit, fearing, I suppose, that they might not be paid. I regret that any shopping we did would have to be...what is the expression? Paid on the nail?"

Despite her mortification, Elizabeth could see that his expression did not alter from one of polite interest, and while she was glad that neither Miss Bingley nor Mrs. Hurst had heard, she felt that the captain at least could be trusted with her confidences.

"Then I shall accompany you all and draw on my London bank. Perhaps

Miss Bennet would feel able to accompany you, and we would not have to take a maid along too. My sister is, as you have seen, exceedingly shy, and I fear she has enjoyed too few such frivolous outings."

"Then, sir, I should be delighted to take your sister shopping, although I fear you may have to resign yourself to several dull hours at the King's Head while we three enjoy ourselves at your expense."

Captain Darcy smiled, a most becoming expression, and they sat in companionable silence while Mr. Bingley's sisters attempted to outdo each other in execution on the fortepiano. Indeed, in view of the heaviness of Mrs. Hurst's hands and right foot, Elizabeth thought that "execution" was very probably the right word.

In a brief pause between pieces, the captain took the opportunity to ask about Mr. Bennet's illness. There was nothing intrusive about his questioning, merely a genuine and compassionate enquiry.

Elizabeth looked at her hands. "He first took ill in July. I do not know whether you were in England, but the weather in this part of the world was extremely wet. He was caught in a downpour, took cold, and from there grew worse. The doctor says it is pneumonia and there is very little we can do except pray." As her eyes filled with tears, she felt the sofa rock as the captain rose and strode to where the two ladies were preparing for a duet.

"I really must come a little closer," he said. "It is not often we sailors get to hear such first-rate music."

More than a little surprised, Elizabeth placed her hand on the sofa, preparatory to rising and leaving the room in haste, but as she did so, her fingers touched a small bundle of cloth. It was a gentleman's silk handkerchief. As she hurriedly wiped her eyes, she looked up and saw the broad, dark blue back of the captain, standing precisely in the spot that hid Elizabeth from the gaze of everyone else in the room.

The expedition to Hatfield was planned at breakfast the following day, and Elizabeth resigned herself to staying another day and night at Netherfield, a decision rendered easier by the recognition that Jane had not yet quite recovered and would prefer to spend the day quietly.

Captain Darcy set off in a curricle with a groom the moment everything was decided and Elizabeth, Miss Darcy, and a maid followed in the carriage, having first ascertained that Mrs. Darcy, too, preferred to remain indoors.

It was a cold, overcast day, but they were warmly wrapped and well equipped with heated bricks and rugs and passed the time pleasantly, deciding where they would go and what they would purchase. Elizabeth was pleased to find her companion a modest young lady with modest requirements. She shuddered to think what Lydia and Kitty would have demanded had they been in Miss Darcy's position.

They arrived at the King's Head and found Captain Darcy and a room he had ordered for them with hot tea and buttered toast to revive them after their journey. While the maid was fixing Miss Darcy's hair, which had a tendency to escape its pins, the captain took Elizabeth to one side and pressed a purse into her hands. "If this is not enough, pray have word sent to me and I will come and find you." He glanced over at his sister who was giggling with the maid as they both struggled to contain her hair. "Whatever she needs, Miss Bennet, and no expense spared. That coat cannot be warm enough, and surely she needs new boots and…" He smiled ruefully. "I am sure you know better than I what is needed, but please let me press upon you that this is one occasion where economy would be false indeed."

Elizabeth's eyes widened as she peered into the purse. "I assure you, Captain Darcy, there is more than enough here to outfit your sister from top to toe."

"And if she sees any books or music or…or…" He was obviously struggling now. "Paper and pencils for drawing, or anything to divert her during the day, please lay them in too."

Elizabeth, greatly daring, placed a hand on his arm. "Do not worry. I will see she has all the most affectionate brother could wish." He looked a little self-conscious at this and turned away to kiss his sister and wish her joy of the outing.

Luckily it had not come on to rain, as Elizabeth had half-suspected it would, and they bustled along the main street to the draper Mr. Stevenson, who could usually be relied upon to have some ready-made items in stock in addition to all the fabrics, ribbons, and other makings they would require.

Once he realised the nature and extent of the purchases they required, Mr. Stevenson and his wife devoted themselves entirely to Miss Darcy, who appeared to be shyly enjoying the attention although it was some time before Elizabeth could induce her to express an opinion. They only managed to find a single dress for day wear suitable for a young lady of Miss Darcy's age and height, but it was very becoming, a cream-coloured muslin with little sprigs of violets. Where fabric was concerned, they were more fortunate and, despite Miss Darcy's protests that they would not need half of their purchases, bought enough for three more day dresses and two for evening.

Mr. Hitchens, the mercer, produced cloth for a fine warm coat in a handsome, almost naval blue. The boot maker had shoes for indoor use and took the measurements for some half boots, undertaking to call at Netherfield for a final fitting.

Word got around the shopkeepers, and everywhere they went, they were met with eager attention. Stockings, bonnets, gloves, under things, and a fine, warm fur muff. They went back to the King's Head for more tea and some hot soup before venturing out again.

"We will go to Mrs. Cottam to have the fabric made up. She is slightly more expensive than Mrs. Finch in Meryton, but having her nieces with her, she is in a larger way of business and we will get the dresses sooner. We can have the coat made in Meryton, which will ensure we do not cause too much ill feeling, for you can have no idea how easily people in small villages are offended, my dear."

Miss Darcy nodded breathlessly as she trotted beside Elizabeth's determined stride. "Oh, Miss Bennet," she said. "Will you not let me pay for anything? I do have a little money, you know." She was about to say something more when she realised they were passing the bookshop and stationers and stopped dead.

Recognising a fellow reader in the look of ardent curiosity, Elizabeth allowed herself to be persuaded to enter, and they did not come out again for quite half an hour, followed by the shop boy with another parcel for the King's Head.

Mrs. Cottam's house was warm and a little stuffy, and by the time the measuring, fitting, and consulting of pattern books was quite finished, Elizabeth was tired and Miss Darcy was positively exhausted.

"So, shall we say Monday at Netherfield for the first fitting?" said Elizabeth. Mrs. Cottam, enraptured by the arrival of so much hard cash, would probably have agreed to anything Elizabeth suggested.

Once in the cold afternoon air, Miss Darcy revived somewhat and did her best to express her gratitude for all that Elizabeth had done. In her anxiety that Elizabeth understand, she became quite animated, and this, with the colour whipped into her cheeks by the autumnal air, made such a pretty picture that Elizabeth could see how struck the captain was when they bustled into the room at the King's Head. He smiled at Elizabeth as they both watched Georgiana run to thank him, only to stop short when she realised there was another gentleman present.

"Georgiana, Miss Bennet, you must allow me to introduce an old friend and shipmate. Lieutenant Grace, this is my sister Georgiana and her friend Miss Bennet."

Lieutenant Grace was a weather-beaten gentleman, rather older than the captain, with a pleasant face and a somewhat old-fashioned way of dressing, the cuffs of his coat falling well over his hands. As they all sat once more, Elizabeth realised that he was missing some fingers from his left hand. "I had no idea Grace was living in Hatfield," said the captain. "One loses touch with shipmates far too easily."

"I only wish I had known earlier," said the lieutenant in a deep Yorkshire burr. "Mrs. Grace and I would have been so happy to have you to dinner." He glanced at the clock on the mantel. "And talking of Mrs. Grace, I had best be getting home; she will be wondering whatever has happened to me. Miss Darcy, Miss Bennet, your servant."

The two men shook hands. "You have my direction now, sir. I shall expect to hear from you."

"My hand on it, Grace, and my compliments to Mrs. Grace."

It was now quite late, and the roads would be dark, save for a half moon and the stars. After a brief, hot meal, they all, including the captain, climbed back into the carriage, and were wrapped in shawls, given hot bricks for their feet, and were then packed in clean straw, a process that reminded Elizabeth more than a little of storing apples for the winter.

Exhausted by the excitement, Georgiana soon fell asleep with her head on her brother's arm. Tentatively, almost shyly, he put the arm about her and held her against his chest. He was sitting opposite Elizabeth, and the tenderness on his face as he drew the rugs about his sister's shoulders was both affecting and curiously charming. He looked up and saw that Elizabeth had seen him and coloured. "I am beginning to wish I told the ostler not to bother with the lamp," he whispered.

She smiled back at him. "Your secret is safe with me, Captain." The coach rumbled on through the night, and the snores of the maid in the corner soon joined the noise of the wheels. They said nothing more until they were approaching Meryton, when Elizabeth saw him struggling to remove something from his coat pocket.

Eventually he managed to extricate a small box, which he passed over to her. "It is her birthday on Sunday. The jeweller assured me this was suitable. Was he right?"

She opened it to find a beautiful little pearl necklace. Elizabeth closed it and handed it back. "You could not have chosen better," she whispered back and then had to smile at the contortions he had to perform to get the box back into its hiding place.

They were passing Longbourn now, and she turned her head to look out of the window. To her horror, the door was open, light spilling onto the carriage sweep, and a figure in black was descending from a gig.

"Oh, stop the coach, please, stop the coach!"

No sooner had the captain rapped on the roof and the carriage halted than she was out and running towards the house, not waiting for the step to be lowered or the groom to accompany her up the dark road. She lost her footing and almost fell, but righted herself and ran on.

She could see Mrs. Hill start to close the door, but she called out and the housekeeper lifted the lamp to see who it was. "Miss Elizabeth?"

"Is it the doctor? Is it my father?" she called as she reached the front door.

A stranger turned in the hall; he was a tall, portly young man with an oddly shining face, dressed in clerical black with a shovel hat in his hand. "Have I the honour of addressing one of my young cousins?" he intoned, and as breathless and concerned as she was, Elizabeth heard the almost liturgical pomposity in his voice, and her heart sank.

She hurriedly dropped a curtsey and did her best to explain and introduce herself. Unable to wait and see who had called, Mrs. Bennet came into the hall, and for once, Elizabeth was glad of her mother's ability to make five words do the work of one. "Lizzy, what are you doing here? You ought to be at Netherfield with Jane. Oh, I do hope nothing is wrong. She is not worse, is she? Do I need to come at once? Though how I am to get there with the horses at the farm, though of course you must have come by carriage, for surely you did not walk at this time of night!"

All this time, Mr. Collins was standing there, hat in hand, an uneasy social smirk on his face, trying to get a word in. Elizabeth glanced out of the front door, and to her horror, she saw the captain walking up the drive, one of the coach lamps in his hand. For some reason, she could not bear him to hear this commotion. "No, Mama," she broke in, wincing at the rudeness. "I have been to Hatfield with Captain Darcy's sister, and I just called in to see how Papa is doing." Then gesturing towards her perspiring cousin, she added, "And this is Mr. Collins, who has just arrived."

As she had hoped, the introduction served to distract her mother, and she managed to bundle Mrs. Bennet and her cousin into the drawing room just as the captain arrived on the doorstep, looking concerned. From the room behind her, she could hear Mr. Collins intoning his concern for Mr. Bennet, and she turned to Hill, who was still waiting at the door.

"Now, don't you go fretting, Miss Elizabeth," said Hill comfortably. "Your father is no worse and maybe even a little better. He's missing you, o' course, but he's all right for the time being. Now you'd best get back into the carriage before your mother comes looking for you."

Impulsively, Elizabeth leaned forward and kissed the older woman on the cheek. "I'll be home tomorrow, I promise," she said and stepped back out into the night, taking the captain's proffered arm.

"I hope nothing is wrong," he said as they slipped their way up the muddy road towards the coach.

"I really must apologise for dashing out like a madwoman." she replied. "I thought that gentleman was a doctor, and instead it is only my cousin Mr. Collins. I am afraid I rather lost my head."

"Do I take it you and Miss Bennet will be leaving us tomorrow?" he asked as he helped her back into her seat in the carriage. Miss Darcy and the maid were both now awake and hurried to wrap her back up in the shawls and rugs.

"It is time we were getting home. My father is missing me, and my mother will need all the help we can give. I fear I have rather forgotten where my duty lies."

As the coach started up again, Miss Darcy hurried to express her thanks and apologies for having kept her from her home, but the captain merely nodded. "I shall ask Bingley to have the carriage ready for you tomorrow," he said.

They sat in companionable silence as the carriage trundled heavily over the road to Netherfield. Elizabeth was very tired, and however hard she tried, she could not bring her thoughts under good regulation. It was most unfair to judge a man from such a brief meeting, but she could not help suspecting that the new arrival at Longbourn would add little to their family circle. This was the man her father believed she ought to marry; she shivered and drew the shawls more tightly around her shoulders.

Chapter Five

E lizabeth and Jane left Netherfield the next morning, followed by the
insincere pleadings of Mrs. Hurst and Miss Bingley that they must stay
at least another week. However, a much more sincere invitation from
Mr. Bingley ensued, and they agreed to return to Netherfield after services
on Sunday for a small luncheon party in honour of Miss Darcy's birthday.

That invitation—and the fact that Mr. Bingley accompanied them back
to Netherfield on horseback—was probably all that stood between the sisters
and their mother's loudly voiced indignation. By the time Mr. Bingley left,
having refused Mrs. Bennet's invitation to dine in view of all the guests at
Netherfield, that lady had managed to convince herself that a match between
him and Jane was all but complete, and her conversation was dedicated to
working out how soon he would propose and how quickly the wedding
could take place.

Elizabeth attempted to protest that nothing of the sort had been decided
and that nobody could gauge Mr. Bingley's intentions at this early stage
of his acquaintance with Jane, but she found herself curiously reluctant to
remind Mrs. Bennet of the family's current, precarious position.

She and Jane went in to visit their father and found him, if anything, a
little stronger, though complaining of the cold and damp despite the fire
roaring in the hearth. When Jane went to remove her bonnet and coat,
Elizabeth lingered, for she could see that he wished to speak to her.

"I understand you met Mr. Collins last night, my dear," he said. She nodded.
"I wish I had never spoken to you about him," he continued with surprising
vehemence. "The man is nothing but a fool and, what is worse, a fool who

cannot hold his tongue. He has been in here prating about Christian resigna-
tion, as though I have not lain here for the last three months contemplating
what must come. There must be an alternative. There must!" He paused to
cough, his whole body shaking. "I should never have mentioned marrying
him! He is not a man you could respect, never mind love. We must rely on
this Mr. Bingley or perhaps some other gentleman. But you must promise
me..." He could not continue. His man, Jessup, came in to administer the
cordials that gave him a little relief, and Elizabeth slipped out, promising
to return later if her father were well enough.

Elizabeth knew the truth, even if her father refused to recognise it. There
was no alternative, and she could not give him any promise that removed
what might well be her family's only hope of a respectable establishment.

Dinner was unusually quiet that evening. Lydia and Kitty were at their
Aunt Phillips's for the evening, Mary was even less talkative than usual, and
Jane was looking tired and pale. Mr. Collins filled the silence with talk. He
was determined to be pleased with everything, from the dinner itself to the
china on the table, and had not the sensitivity or perhaps the intelligence to
comprehend how this might be seen by the woman whose husband he seemed
about to supplant. When not appearing to gloat over his inheritance, he
spoke in glowing terms of his patron, the Lady Catherine de Bourgh, whom
he described as the pattern of all the amiable virtues, but whom Elizabeth
thought sounded like a bully of the worst sort. "... for there is not a farm,
no, nor a cottage on her estate where she is not thoroughly acquainted with
all their little business, nor one where she has not given the benefit of her
advice and ensured that that advice has been taken in every respect. Indeed,
in my own little rectory, she has completely reorganised the bedrooms and
insisted that I terminate the lease on the glebe land to a farmer of whose
morals and political views she does not approve."

Elizabeth had a vision of herself perpetually curtseying to a woman who
bore a startling resemblance to an older Miss Bingley and had to grit her
teeth not to say something cutting, which he would probably not understand
until later, if at all. Jane kept her eyes on her plate most of the evening and
retired early, pleading a headache; Mary rushed out with her, and Elizabeth was left to keep the peace between an oblivious Mr. Collins and an
increasingly irritated Mrs. Bennet.

The next day was more of the same. Mr. Bennet, who had invited the man there in the first place, could stand very little of his company and soon packed him off with Mr. Lester, the steward, to view the estate. That gentleman, who had originally hoped for a permanent position with Mr. Bennet's heir, soon realised that any such post would be insupportable and revenged himself by dragging Mr. Collins through every slough and mire in the neighbourhood. When the clergyman eventually arrived home, he climbed from the gig, mud to the eyebrows and frozen to the bone.

After a subdued dinner, Elizabeth cut short his conversation by suggesting he read to them all. However, his choice of *Night Thoughts* by Edward Young soon reduced them all to such low spirits that they were glad to retire early to escape him. Elizabeth was the last to go to bed, having called in to the kitchen at her mother's request to check on the morning's breakfast. As she went past Mary's little room, the door, which was difficult to latch properly, swung open to reveal Mary on her knees beside the bed.

Mary looked up as the door opened, and Elizabeth was shocked to see her sister, blinking myopically, her cheeks wet with tears. She slipped in quickly and shut the door. Mary wiped her eyes with her fingers and looked around for her spectacles, which Elizabeth found on her dresser and handed to her.

"Can you tell me what is wrong, dear?" she asked softly.

Mary, who had seemed to regain her equilibrium, burst into tears once more and flung herself into Elizabeth's arms. "Kitty and Lydia say I ought to marry Mr. Collins," she sobbed. "And if I do not, we shall all be poor, but I cannot, Lizzy, I cannot!"

"Why should you have to marry Mr. Collins?" asked Elizabeth, glad that that gentleman was quartered at the other end of the house.

"They say it is because I am dull, like he is, and because I like reading sermons and…and…conduct books. But that's only because I want to know what's right, but, Lizzy, I cannot marry him. I cannot. His hands are all wet, and Lydia told me about babies, and I cannot do that with Mr. Collins! I cannot!"

No, you cannot. But I may have to. Shaking herself, Elizabeth looked down at the younger girl in her arms and realised that she and Jane had left Mary too much to her own devices. With no one to guide her, a father who ignored her, and a mother who did not understand her, Mary had tried to make her own path and, not surprisingly, had made a poor fist of it. She hugged her sister and tried to reassure her.

"No, dear," she said. "Lydia and Kitty are just being thoughtless as usual. Nobody with sense believes you ought to marry Mr. Collins, and you should put it out of your mind once and for all."

It took her some time to calm Mary, and by the time Elizabeth retired for the night, Jane was fast asleep, and she was left alone with her thoughts. It was very late before she finally managed to sleep herself, and her dreams were distressing, so that she woke next day feeling tense and unrefreshed.

The next day was Sunday, so they all, including Mr. Collins, turned out in their Sunday best for church. There was an uncommon show of bonnets all round, for many young and, indeed, not-so-young ladies were not immune to the prospect of new visitors to the neighbourhood, especially new neighbours who could be expected to wear fine red coats. However, to the general disappointment, the only officer from the militia present was an elderly major and his equally elderly wife.

The arrival of the party from Netherfield went a little way to relieve matters. Miss Bingley and Mrs. Hurst swept into church, both looking disagreeable despite the fact that they must have realised their dresses cost twice that of any other lady present. Mr. Bingley, on the other hand, looked amiable and rather dashing in a coat of dark green.

The main attraction, however, was undoubtedly Captain Darcy, who had come in uniform with his sister blushing shyly on his arm. Two equally undoubtable sailors completed the party, looking particularly gallant in their best shore-going rigs with bright red waistcoats and watchet blue jackets. Although the sailors took seats at the back, they and the captain were obviously accustomed to the service and made a very fine sound in the psalms and the closing hymn.

Mr. Collins was no more immune to curiosity than was any other member of the congregation, and as they left, he wanted to know the names of all the party. When he learned who the captain and his sister were, he swept into action. "Why, that must be the Captain Darcy who is nephew to Lady Catherine. I must go and introduce myself and assure him of her Ladyship's health and well being."

Elizabeth was alarmed. "Cousin, surely there can be no need of such attentions to a gentleman to whom you have not been introduced?"

"My office gives me licence where the mere layman must hold back," replied Mr. Collins before he bustled forward. Elizabeth could not bear to watch and turned away to talk to Lady Lucas, who was enquiring after her father. She could not, however, avoid seeing the captain looking at her cousin with surprise as Mr. Collins writhed himself into a position much more self-abasing than the ordinary bow between gentlemen. She could not hear what he was saying and was heartily glad of the fact.

By the time they got outside, Mr. Bingley and his sisters had already left in one carriage, while the captain and Miss Darcy waited to take Elizabeth and Jane in another. For once, Kitty and Lydia's desire to be away from church as soon as possible had worked in everyone's favour, for Mr. Collins and their mother, not forgetting Mary, had all disappeared.

As they approached the carriage, they saw the captain toss the sailors a coin. "That's to drink to my sister's health. Liberty until four bells, first watch. Do not come back disguised and no fighting with the lobsters." They knuckled their foreheads cheerfully and headed off for the village, no doubt to find the nearest tavern.

The party in the carriage was equally cheerful. By no doubt Herculean efforts, Miss Darcy had been supplied with a new dress, spencer, and half boots, and she was innocently pleased with her appearance. Back at Netherfield, even Miss Bingley laid herself out to be agreeable, and the birthday presents were received with becoming excitement and gratitude.

Elizabeth and Jane had racked their brains to think of something suitable—and inexpensive—and their choice of a bottle of their own lavender water in a netted purse, originally made by Jane as a Christmas present for Aunt Gardiner, looked very well when wrapped in a clean handkerchief and tied with a ribbon. The pearl necklace from her brother was, however, quite properly the highlight of Miss Darcy's day.

After the meal, they retired to the drawing room, and Miss Darcy was persuaded to play, quickly revealing herself as by far the most accomplished musician of the party. As her brother watched proudly, she revealed a skill in execution and a lightness of touch Elizabeth had seldom heard from an amateur, and the applause when she finished was hearty and well deserved.

She was pleased to see that Mr. Bingley spent much of his time with Jane, and once Elizabeth had discreetly nudged her sister into showing some little pleasure at his attentions, the two of them were soon heads together in conversation. Miss Bingley and Mrs. Hurst both looked as though they wished to interrupt, so Elizabeth engaged them in conversation about the past Season in Town. As she had suspected, the temptation to show away to a mere country bumpkin was sufficient to distract them from interfering with what she hoped was her sister's courtship.

Despite having to listen to a lot of talk about people she had never met and would never wish to, the afternoon passed pleasantly with music and conversation. Even Mrs. Darcy eventually drifted over to thank Elizabeth for taking her daughter shopping. "For I know her clothes were not what they ought to have been, but I could never persuade Mr. Darcy that girls do grow so at Georgiana's age, and one cannot be always letting down hems and tucks." Her voice was thin and querulous, and her sentences hardly seemed to have an end, merely gliding endlessly one into another. "For you would hardly credit that she was such a little girl until quite recently, and then suddenly she was taller than me, and he was always saying it was a great nonsense to say so, but surely he could see for himself, but perhaps not, for he would not see her from one week to the next…" It was only the offer of a cup of tea and a piece of cake, both of which she consumed greedily, that finally allowed Elizabeth to escape.

Eventually the time came to leave. Despite entreaties from Mr. Bingley, warmly supported by Miss Darcy, Elizabeth and Jane were both adamant that they had to get back to Longbourn before it grew very late. In any event, the Netherfield ball was planned for the following weekend, and they would all meet again then.

As Elizabeth and Jane stood in the hall, waiting for the carriage to come round, they were all surprised to hear hoof beats speedily approaching the house. Their original fear, that it was bad news from Longbourn, was soon dispelled when they saw the red uniform. "It's a militiaman," said Mr. Bingley in amazement.

Captain Darcy behind him soon set him right. "No," he said. "It's a marine." His face was stern, and the hand that Elizabeth could see was clenched by his side.

The soldier dismounted before the house and saluted. "Cap'n Darcy?" he inquired.

"Here." A long envelope was handed over, and the captain ripped it apart, scanning the contents.

"Fitzwilliam?" It was Miss Darcy, timidly touching his sleeve. "Is it?"

"Yes, dear," he said. "I am afraid it is. I am ordered to sea within the month."

Chapter Six

M iss Darcy gave a small cry of distress. "We do not have to go back, do we?" she said and then burst out, "You promised!"

He turned quickly and covered her hands with his. "I promise, sweetheart, you shall not have to go back. Now you must return to the drawing room before you catch cold. I shall see the ladies off, and then we shall have a council of war." When she looked doubtful, he kissed her forehead, turned her round, and pushed her very gently towards the room they had just left. "Off you go."

He watched until the door closed behind her. "Bingley," he said hoarsely. "Your arm, if you please." Mr. Bingley leapt to his aid and helped him to sit down in one of the hall chairs. "Can you put the man up for the night? He can return to London with me in the morning; I must go and see my attorney at once."

"Of course I can." Bingley nodded to the butler who went to give the marine directions to the stables. "But are you sure you're in any state to travel?"

"I will be well in a few minutes. It does not seem to last as long anymore as it did once. Would you be a good chap and ask Georgie to meet me in the library? Then when she has left, perhaps one of your hands could help me upstairs. I shall have a brief caulk and be right as rain within the hour." He kept his eyes closed but turned his head to where Elizabeth and Jane had been standing. "I apologise for not rising, ladies, and shall hope to see you both at Bingley's ball."

The coach arrived at that moment, and after a somewhat confused leave-taking, Elizabeth and Jane were driven away. Elizabeth at least was somewhat worried; not only were they about to lose an agreeable new acquaintance to the exigencies of war, but the gentleman was, despite his protestations, quite obviously unwell. She wondered whether the superiors who gave him his orders knew of his condition. It all seemed terribly unfair, especially as his sister and her mother were for some reason dependent upon him.

It was cold despite the rugs, and the two sisters huddled together under the coach blankets. Jane hid her face in her muffler, and Elizabeth resolved to wait until they got back to Longbourn to question her. The rest of the journey passed in silence, save for the moment just outside Longbourn when they heard two voices raised in song on the road, and realised that they had just passed the two sailors returning to Netherfield. As they climbed out of the carriage, Elizabeth called out to the coachman, asking him whether he would be kind enough to take up the two men on the way back, "for it is a cold night, and it looks as though it might rain." The coachman touched his hat and agreed.

After an excellent luncheon and tea at Netherfield, neither was inclined to dine; in any case, Mrs. Bennet had not expected them back, and there was nothing prepared for them. So they contented themselves with a cup of tea while everyone else was at dinner and Elizabeth could finally ask Jane for her news.

Jane sighed. "Mr. Bingley is very agreeable, and he certainly feels as he ought with regard to his duties to the estate," she said. "If it were not for poor Papa, I am sure we could in time come to an understanding, but the fact remains that there is no time. I feel as though I ought to draw him on somehow and have not the remotest idea how to do so." The two sisters sat in silence for a time before Jane continued. "He is, I am sure, a good man; whether or not he is the *right* man, I cannot tell, but I am well aware that it is my duty to marry him if I possibly can."

There was nothing Elizabeth could say to this and, while she deprecated the change in Jane, she could hardly quarrel with her conclusions. Whether Jane had yet realised her sister's possible fate, Elizabeth did not know, and she was certainly not going to be the one to enlighten her.

They both managed to spend the rest of the evening with their father, Jane in reading to him and Elizabeth seeing to some neglected correspondence. They had the satisfaction of seeing him more settled than he had been for some time, although he continued weak. Elizabeth missed the caustic humour that had once been so evident. She had often wished that he would not sharpen his wits on his neighbours and family, but its disappearance underlined how changed he was by his illness, and she wished with all her heart that she could hear him describe Mr. Collins with all the acerbity that had once been his.

That night, as she listened to her sister breathing in sleep, Elizabeth lay awake remembering the scene in the hall at Netherfield, the captain sitting with his head back, the white of his stock and the paleness of his face against the dark wood of the wainscoting. It seemed most unfair that such a gallant gentleman was obliged to return to sea before he was wholly recovered. It spoke well of him that he was nevertheless prepared to do his duty.

The next day, the house was set upon its ears by Mr. Collins who was—or fancied himself to be—ill. The apothecary was sent for, the details of his digestion discussed in public and at length, and Elizabeth scarcely knew which was more annoying: Mr. Collins's complaints or her mother's angry rejection of the suggestion that he might have eaten something unwholesome "… for we are all perfectly well, and it is a great nonsense to think that anything in my kitchen would have singled out Mr. Collins."

"Perhaps Cook has poisoned him," suggested Lydia. "And I am sure I do not blame her, for he has been perfectly horrid since he got here." Her sisters cried out at the suggestion, but Lydia was not to be silenced. "As far as I am concerned, if I could find a way to do so without being caught, I should be tempted to do it myself."

"Lydia, if you cannot say anything sensible, you had better go visit your Aunt Phillips," said Mrs. Bennet. Elizabeth reflected that this was all apiece with her mother's idea of controlling her wayward younger daughters: rewarding them for behaving badly by sending them where they were anxious to go.

The weather had turned fine again, and she hoped the captain would have good roads all the way into London. When it came on to rain towards evening, she could not help worrying just a little.

Luckily, Mr. Collins kept to his bed for several days, and while this caused a great deal of inconvenience to the household, it was agreed by everybody, albeit tacitly, that this was preferable to his company. The two youngest sisters, when not visiting their friends in Meryton, were consumed with preparation for the ball, rumour having running riot as to the arrangements and their probable cost.

Mrs. Needham had told Sukey who told Mrs. Phillips that all the militia officers were invited, as was half the county, a band had been brought from London at enormous expense, there were to be ices and French champagne and enough white soup to float a man o' war, Mrs. Hurst's gown had cost a hundred guineas, and Miss Bingley's had cost two hundred—at which point Elizabeth had refused to believe another word. She contented herself with refurbishing her old gown with some ribbons Aunt Gardiner had sent from London and with stitching the soles back onto her old dancing shoes. It would have been a great waste of money to do more, but one did not want to look like a complete antidote.

The ball was set for the full moon on Saturday, and the family coach and horses were prepared. To everyone's dismay, Mr. Collins had recovered from his indisposition and squeezed his way amongst his "fair cousins," for as he said, "Lady Catherine says that dancing in respectable company is a perfectly acceptable activity for a clergyman, being both healthful and tending to restrain the company from light speech and overly high spirits." As they were removing their wraps in the withdrawing room at Netherfield, Elizabeth remarked to Jane that he gave one a very clear picture of the entertainments countenanced by that august lady.

While rumour had inevitably exaggerated the scale of the arrangements, they were nevertheless more lavish than usual for the neighbourhood. The rooms were full of light and hothouse flowers, the wine was much better than they were used to, and the band in quite another class from the one they had all heard at too many assemblies.

Mr. Bingley immediately solicited Jane's hand for the first dance, and they opened the proceedings in fine style. Elizabeth looked round for the captain and Miss Darcy, and she was eventually reduced to asking Miss Bingley. "The captain is about somewhere, but he thinks his sister too young to be out." Unfortunately, at that moment Lydia and Kitty could be heard roaring with laughter in a group of young officers, and Miss Bingley's expression said everything she was perhaps still too well brought up to say aloud.

Elizabeth said nothing. She was about to go and attempt to restrain her sisters when Mr. Collins arrived and asked to be her partner in the next set. There was no way she could avoid the invitation, and so did her best to accept politely. To her horror, he seemed to be adopting an almost proprietary manner towards her. Her mother had begun, over the past few days, to speculate whether he would get round to choosing one of her daughters and had taken it upon herself to warn him away from Jane. Elizabeth wondered whether Mrs. Bennet had finally decided it was her duty to nudge him in Elizabeth's direction. While they stood waiting for the next set to begin, Mr. Collins favoured Elizabeth with his views of the current state of the war and the political situation, interspersed with awkward compliments to herself and her family. She did her best to listen politely, but her attention kept wandering, and she had to prevent herself from looking around for the captain.

Mr. Collins could not dance, which was bad enough, but what was worse was that he could not accept direction without apologising at length, which sent him further astray in the set. Elizabeth could see Mrs. Hurst and Miss Bingley, heads together, enjoying her predicament, so she set her teeth, held her head high, and did her best to carry the situation off with an air.

During one evolution of the dance in which Mr. Collins, having led with the wrong hand, had then gone the wrong way up the set and had to be called back, she saw her mother and Lady Lucas sitting together, her mother looking extremely pleased with herself, and she knew that, to Mrs. Bennet at least, her marriage was as good as made. Since Mrs. Bennet's wishes soon became Mrs. Bennet's facts, Elizabeth had no doubt that the neighbourhood were all being told that the Bennets' fortunes had been saved. A slightly soiled glove met hers, and she suppressed a shudder.

Down the dance, she saw the captain standing near the fireplace, talking, or at least listening, to Sir William. The captain was wearing his green spectacles again, and she could not see his eyes, which was a pity for they were quite his most striking feature. She hoped he was not unwell. She would have liked a word with him, but Mr. Collins seemed determined to monopolise her company. As she stood up with him for the next dance, she had to listen to his breathless comparisons between Netherfield and Lady Catherine's seat, Rosings. "For although the pictures here are very fine, they are nothing compared to those at Rosings. The portrait of the late Sir Lewis de Bourgh cost over three hundred guineas and..." There was much more of this. Every time the pattern brought them back together, he seemed to have another comment to the detriment of Netherfield and the aggrandisement of Rosings.

There were more candles than she had ever seen in one place, and the room grew increasingly hot. Frantically, she tried to form an excuse to get away from her cousin. The set was coming to an end, and she knew that, if she did not think of something, she would be unable to avoid his company for supper as well. The music ended, the couples exchanged bows and curtsies, and she had thought of nothing. She saw her cousin open his mouth, but to her utmost relief, she heard a familiar deep voice at her side.

"May I have the pleasure of the next set, Miss Elizabeth?" It was Captain Darcy, looking composed and elegant.

Something unknotted in her chest, and she dropped him a grateful curtsey. "I should be delighted, sir," she said.

Chapter Seven

Elizabeth took his hand, and they threaded their way through to a position halfway down and waited for the music to begin. She could see Mr. Collins watching her with a strange expression, combining his usual, awkward social smirk with a distinctly thwarted look. She hurriedly turned her attention to her partner.

"I had hoped to see Miss Darcy tonight," she said.

He smiled. "She is only fifteen and not at all accustomed to large social gatherings. When I proposed that she not attend, she was only too grateful to stay upstairs with her mother."

The music began, and they exchanged bows. Elizabeth suddenly felt happier than she had in weeks. Her life was fraught with difficulties that would soon come to a head, but she did not have to think about that now. The music was lively, her partner handsome and considerate, and when she caught sight of her own reflection in the great mirror over the fireplace, she thought she looked as well as she ever had in her life. They joined hands, his warm and firm, the scar on his wrist evidence of a life of energy and adventure, and she smiled up at him brilliantly.

They parted, proceeded down the set, and met again at the bottom. She thought of asking him whether he were still to leave shortly and swiftly decided not to. There was a strange bubbling sensation under her ribcage, her heart was beating fast, and she had no desire to dampen the mood. "You can have no idea," she said, "how pleasant it is to have a partner who knows what he is about."

"You can thank my sister and Mrs. Hurst," he replied, extending a hand for her to take. "I only knew two dances: the two I danced at the assembly. They assured me that was not nearly enough and drilled me most severely all yesterday afternoon. They were more exacting than any admiral." They changed hands and turned in the opposite direction.

"Then I must thank them both next time I see them," she said as they processed up the room. Mr. Bingley was not dancing this time, and she could see him at the door, talking to one of the servants.

"Miss Bingley is to be congratulated. This evening will be talked about for months."

"Not least by Miss Bingley," he replied blandly as they parted and led down the set again. When they met at the bottom of the room, he looked a little penitent. "I really ought not to make a game of my hostess. It is the most terrible return for her hospitality to me and my little family."

"Sir," she replied, "I promise to tell no one. I know too well the impulse to say something true regardless of whether or not it is kind or polite. Usually I manage to restrain myself, but sometimes the thing is just too true to swallow. One can only hope for a friend to tell who will be too much a friend to tell someone else." He managed to bow his assent without losing either his place or his rhythm and another wave of happiness washed over her. He really was a remarkably good-looking man. His skin still held the remnants of a tan, no doubt acquired in foreign parts; the small scar that bisected his left eyebrow was, if anything, faintly dashing; and despite those horrible green spectacles, the face beneath them was manly and well formed.

The pair in front of them stumbled when Miss Goulding caught her heel in the hem of her gown. The captain seized her arm before she fell, set her gently on her feet, and resumed his place, all without losing his step. "Bravo, sir," said Elizabeth gaily. "Saviour of the nation and of the dance!"

"Believe me, Miss Bennet, there is nothing like a few years at sea to teach a man to keep his feet in all weathers. By the time I had been at sea six months, I had broken an arm and lost two teeth, although thankfully only the milk kind."

"You must have gone to sea very young."

"I was nine." He must have spotted her dismay for he continued, "You are quite correct; that is far too young. Now I am captain, I will not take a young gentleman aboard without he is at least twelve or thirteen and only then if I am persuaded it is his earnest desire to go to sea. One sees too many lads made miserable by a life they have not chosen and for which they are not sufficiently strong." His face had become stern, but by the time they met again at the foot of the set, he had quite obviously set aside any gloomy reflections. "I was hoping to beg for your company at supper. I trust I have not been forestalled by any earlier applicants."

"I would be delighted to join you for supper," she said, and her heart sang.

The set ended, and during the polite ripple of applause, Mr. Bingley came over to them. "I am sorry to interrupt, but if I might have a word with you, Darcy? Miss Elizabeth, your servant." They bowed to her and moved to one side of the room for a brief conversation. Elizabeth, slightly surprised by this, resolved to seek out Kitty and Lydia to make sure all was well. She had scarcely reached the door when Mr. Bingley and the captain came after her.

"I am sorry to be the bearer of bad news," said Mr. Bingley, "but a servant has come from Longbourn. Your father is not at all well."

Elizabeth went cold, her recent happiness cut off as though with a knife. "We must go home."

"I have arranged for my coach to come round," said Mr. Bingley. "And it occurs to Darcy and me that, if you and Mrs. Bennet leave now, your sisters can follow later in your own carriage with Mr. Collins as escort. Darcy here has volunteered to return with you now in case there is any assistance he or Netherfield can offer."

Elizabeth could hardly think. "Sir, that is most kind, but—"

"But nothing," replied the captain firmly. "I have seen plenty of sickness aboard, and you do not know but what another pair of hands might be needed. The younger girls will, I dare say, only become distressed without being of much help, and I cannot believe that Mr. Collins—that is to say, your cousin is better employed bringing them home in an hour or so."

Through the open door, Elizabeth could see the carriage coming round. Mrs. Bennet came bustling out of the card room, followed by Mrs. Hurst, who must have informed her. "Oh, Lizzy, whatever are we to do? We must all return to Longbourn at once—your poor dear father, I ought never to have left him. Has anyone sent for Doctor Wallace?"

A servant arrived carrying their wraps and a huge greatcoat for the captain. Elizabeth did her best to explain as she bundled her mother up warmly and then hurried her into the coach. Her mother was, to her surprise, quick to see at least one advantage of the arrangement. "For it would never do for Mr.

Collins to know how ill your father is before he has to. It is quite bad enough to see him pricing up my furniture without that!" Elizabeth, mortified at such comments before the captain, did her best to turn the conversation. Mrs. Bennet, however, was not to be gainsaid.

"I do hope Hill has sent for Doctor Wallace, for even though he costs so very much, I am sure he is the only one who has done your father any good at all, and that is little enough. It is all very well the doctor saying he needs to move somewhere warm, but we cannot all possibly move, and where would we go? That wicked Napoleon has quite overrun Europe, and though to be sure your father has often said he wished to visit Greece, how on earth would we get there?" She was obviously talking more or less at random, her hands twisting under her shawl. "And should he die, what would become of us?" She raised her head and looked at Elizabeth accusingly. "If you had only secured Mr. Collins, we should all have had somewhere to go, and now I do not know what we shall do if Mr. Collins does not marry you and Mr. Bingley does not marry Jane."

Elizabeth, tried beyond endurance, interrupted. "Mama, please, surely we can talk of all this another time. We need not assume the worst until we see how my father is doing when we get home." Mrs. Bennet, recalled to her better nature, filled the rest of the journey with her hopes and fears for her husband's health.

When they arrived at Longbourn, they found the house lit up. The door was flung open before the carriage stopped. As they entered the house, they could hear Mr. Bennet in his library. The deep, rattling cough they had hoped was gone was audible from the hallway. Mrs. Bennet and Elizabeth hurried in to discover him lying on his usual couch, his nightshirt gaping at the throat, his arms flailing weakly as he fought for breath.

"Is there any coffee in the house?" Elizabeth had quite forgotten that Captain Darcy was present until he spoke.

"Yes, sir," answered Hill, absently responding to the voice of authority. She had knelt beside the couch where she was attempting to cool Mr. Bennet's forehead with damp cloths.

"Then have some made up at once, as strong as may be, and we must get the gentleman sitting up."

Captain Darcy stripped off his heavy coat and flung it into a chair. Ignoring the servants standing round, he went and bent over the couch. "Good evening, sir. My name is Darcy. I brought your wife and Miss Elizabeth back from Netherfield," he said. "I am going to lift you up so you can breathe more easily." With that, he placed a strong arm under Mr. Bennet's back and lifted him gently into a sitting position. "Open that window! He needs air more than he needs warmth."

The open window brought a cold wind that fluttered the candles and fanned the fire in the hearth. There were bowls about the room from where the patient had vomited. "Clear all this away, and hurry with that coffee." He turned to Elizabeth. "If there are wax candles, they will be better for him than all this tallow."

This, at least, Mrs. Bennet understood. "There! And I told him it was false economy, but no, he would not listen and insisted." Elizabeth hurried her out of the room.

"Mama, you had best go change out of your good gown. The captain and I will see to my father until you come down again." She knew that with Hill occupied in the library and Sarah in the kitchen, it would be some time before her mother could come back, as she would have to change unassisted. As Mrs. Bennet bustled upstairs, Elizabeth hurried to the kitchen where the best candles were kept.

When she returned, she found the door shut and Hill on duty outside. "The gentleman and Jessup are putting your father into a clean nightshirt. We shall have to wait." The coffee arrived shortly afterwards and was passed thought the door.

Mrs. Bennet came down but went back upstairs at once. "I am sure my nerves will not stand this waiting around. Lizzy, you will call me if anything happens."

Elizabeth was almost dancing with impatience by the time the door opened again, but she could see that the situation had changed for the better. Her father, though pale and exhausted, was breathing much more easily, and the cough that still racked his frame did not, at least to her, appear to be as strong. The window was still open and the air, though cold, was clean and fresh. The heavy blankets about his shoulders apparently protected him from the worst of the chill.

When he saw Elizabeth, he held out his hand. "I am sorry to have spoiled your pleasure, child." His voice was hoarse.

"I am sorry to find you so unwell, sir." She dropped to her knees beside him.

"I am feeling more than a little foolish now, for I was sure…my last hour had come."

"I am afraid you cannot be spared just yet awhile," she replied. His eyes were drifting shut, even as he coughed, so she kissed his forehead, and they tiptoed from the room, leaving Jessup to replace the candles and keep watch. Elizabeth turned to Captain Darcy. "We are deeply indebted to you, sir," she said. "How did you know what to do?"

"I had a shipmate afflicted with a terrible cough, poor fellow, every time we exercised the guns and the ship filled with smoke. Strong coffee was the only thing that helped him, and I thought it might do the same here. Come—you must sit down; you look exhausted."

"Just for a moment, then, for I must go and inform Mama what has happened and make ready for Doctor Wallace, though indeed there seems very little for him to do now. I wonder that he has not tried coffee himself."

"I am afraid the effects are not long lasting, and our surgeon, Mr. Luscombe, always says coffee puts a strain on the heart if used to excess. However, since Mr. Bennet was having difficulty breathing, I thought it well worth the attempt."

"Indeed it was, sir." Having sat down, Elizabeth was starting to feel extremely tired. "I am afraid I am too tired and flustered to say everything I ought, but I am very grateful. We all are."

"Pray, think nothing of it, Miss Elizabeth. Now, if you wish to go and tell your mother, I will wait here for the doctor."

It took a long time to calm and reassure her mother, and when that was done, Mrs. Bennet retired for the night, Sarah at last being released from the sickroom. When Elizabeth came down, Doctor Wallace was with her father, and he did not come out of the room until the Longbourn carriage arrived from Netherfield. Jane in particular was consumed with anxiety for her father, and even Kitty and Lydia were frightened into something resembling a respectful silence.

Mr. Collins seemed torn between resentment at having been excluded from the events of the evening and gratification that Lady Catherine's nephew had condescended to assist. His confused attempt to express his gratitude only succeeded in angering Elizabeth and astonishing the captain, who stood looking down on the shorter man as though at some curiosity in a museum.

Elizabeth, in all the bustle, managed a brief word with Doctor Wallace.

"I do not apprehend any immediate danger," said the doctor in his blunt Scottish way. "However, he cannot be said to be improving, nor can I see any hope of such improvement before the good weather comes, if indeed his strength lasts that long." And with that, he climbed heavily into his gig and trotted off into the night.

It seemed to take an age to persuade everyone to retire. Once assured that the worst had not happened, Kitty and Lydia were full of the ball, and even Mary had apparently enjoyed herself more than usual. Elizabeth had to shoo them upstairs to continue the conversation in their rooms. Jane seemed tired and pensive, and Mr. Collins admitted to some fatigue and eventually drifted off to bed.

Elizabeth went into the library for one last check on her father and was startled to see Captain Darcy sitting beside him. He rose as she entered the room. "Your father's man has just gone to see to his chamber," he whispered. "I agreed to stay here until he gets back."

"Surely, Mr. Hill, our manservant, came back with the doctor?"

"He was caught in a shower on the way there. I sent him to shift his clothes." They sat for a moment in silence, watching the rise and fall of Mr. Bennet's chest, both noting the unmistakable hitch in his breathing.

"I cannot thank you enough, Captain Darcy. I do not know what we would have done without you."

"I have every confidence that you would have managed, Miss Elizabeth. I have always considered you a very capable young lady."

She smiled. "Not the compliment a lady expects from a dancing partner, but welcome none the less."

"It is nothing less than the truth; I assure you."

Jessup and Mr. Hill appeared at the door, and Elizabeth and the captain left the room, the captain picking up his greatcoat as he went. The horses from Netherfield were being walked outside, and at his hail, the coachman hurried to hitch them up once more.

"With your permission, I shall call tomorrow to see how your father does."

"You will be very welcome." She remained while he climbed into the coach and it was driven away. She watched until it disappeared from view among the trees then finally closed and bolted the great front door.

Chapter Eight

By ten o'clock next morning, Elizabeth was persuaded that her period of grace was about to expire. Mrs. Bennet was late down for breakfast, and Mr. Collins did not appear at all, but there was an air of determination about her mother, and when Elizabeth heard her telling Hill to ask Mr. Collins to come and meet her in the back parlour as soon as he came down, there was little doubt in her mind as to the probable subject of their conversation.

The sun was out, and while it was cold, it was at least not raining, and Elizabeth decided to seize the chance for a little outdoor exercise while she yet could. She was just about to leave the garden by the gate to the wood, when she saw the Netherfield carriage arrive and Captain Darcy, supported by one of his sailors, climb out and seek admission to the house. By the time she had removed her coat and outdoor boots, the captain had been admitted to the library, the sailor remaining seated in the hall, his broad-brimmed hat with a ribbon reading "Achilles" about it, resting on his knees.

She could hear the sound of men's voices from within and thought about joining them. However, unwilling to fatigue her father with too many visitors at once, she went into the parlour instead and started on the household accounts, which had been somewhat neglected of late. She felt oddly nervous, and although she would have scorned to listen at the door, she found herself trying to catch some sense of the conversation from the tone of their voices. This, as she told herself impatiently, was ridiculous, even if she could distinguish the captain's deeper tones from her father's husky baritone. At least her father's cough seemed to be under control this morning. Firmly, she turned her attention to the bill for sea coal, which would have been excessive if it had not been essential to keep the fires burning for her father.

She was so engrossed in her search for an errant two shillings and eleven pence, three farthings, that at first she did not hear Mr. Hill coughing to attract her attention. Startled, she raised her head and then got to her feet as he announced, "Captain Darcy to see you, Miss Elizabeth."

He came into the room, resting on the arm of his man, and bowed carefully. "Good morning," he said. "I have your father's permission for a private meeting with you, and if I may have your permission to sit, perhaps Anderssen might have a whet in your kitchen while we talk."

"Of course you may sit, Captain," she replied, somewhat flustered. "Perhaps this seat here? Hill, will you see to the captain's man?" A sudden heat flowed all over her, and to her astonishment, her hands were shaking.

It was obvious that the captain was once more suffering from whatever ailed him, for he needed the assistance of his man to find the chair and, once seated in it, had to sit with his eyes shut for a few moments before recovering something of his colour.

"Is there anything I can get you? A brandy perhaps?" she asked, but he smiled and shook his head, only to wince as this obviously exacerbated his condition.

"I apologise for coming to see you in this state," he began. "However, after last night, I thought it as well not to waste any time." He took a deep breath, opened his eyes, and sought her gaze with his, removing the green spectacles and tucking them into a pocket. "Pray forgive me if I encroach on matters you would prefer to keep private, Miss Elizabeth, but it seems that we are both in something of a predicament, and it occurs to me that, in helping you, I would also greatly assist myself and vice versa."

Elizabeth began to feel a little sick. Her mother's indiscretions of the previous evening had obviously caused the captain to see her as some sort of charity case. She opened her mouth to protest that she required no such pity, when his next sentence silenced her entirely.

"You have probably gathered that I was obliged to remove my sister from my brother's care at very short notice. To put it bluntly, and I beg your pardon for being obliged to do so, when I got to Pemberley, I found that he had turned it into something not very far from a...a...*disorderly house*. Never an abstemious man, he is now a confirmed drunkard. Never a generous man, he might now be considered almost a miser. Never an affectionate man, he has treated my poor sister and her mother as little better than unwanted lodgers."

He sighed and looked down. "In all this, he is, I regret to say, accompanied and encouraged by the local clergyman. This man was my father's godson, and he owes his position entirely to a legacy in his will. Not content with joining my brother in his debauchery, he has so wormed himself into my brother's affections that he has persuaded him that it would be an excellent *joke* to marry my sister to this Mr. Wickham and split her fortune of £20,000 between them, regardless of my sister's wishes in the matter."

Elizabeth gasped in horror. He looked up at her, and she could see his distress. "You have met Mrs. Darcy. I can conceive of no one less likely to prevent such a match. Moreover, my father, having little respect for her understanding, ignored her as a trustee for her daughter's fortune, appointing instead my brother and my cousin, who is currently abroad with his regiment. While I doubt that Colonel Fitzwilliam would consent to such a match in advance, if presented with a *fait accompli,* he would have little alternative save to agree to the release of her fortune to her husband.

"I have begun proceedings to have my sister declared a Ward in Chancery, so that my brother would have no further influence over her." Until now, his voice had been firm and almost dispassionate, but for the first time, he sounded uncomfortable. "It has been represented to me that I would have a much better chance of obtaining custody of my sister's person if I had a family home in which to accommodate her. As a bachelor, I am in no better state than my brother when considered as a guardian. Any interview with her mother would soon reveal her unfitness to be charged with Georgiana's welfare while I am at sea."

While horrified by the narrowly averted fate of a young lady she had come to consider as a friend, Elizabeth had no idea what he expected her to do. Surely, he was not offering her a position as companion or housekeeper?

"I understood last night from your mother that you were expecting to receive an offer from Mr. Collins. Your father informs me that no such offer has yet been made, and I wonder whether you would consider me as a husband instead."

She could almost feel the colour draining from her cheeks. Whatever she had been expecting, it had not been this.

"I admit that I cannot offer you Longbourn," he continued. "However, I

have been fortunate with prize money. I could settle £10,000 on you immediately, for your own use, with say another £5,000 if I get knocked on the
head. This would surely be enough for you to support your mother and sisters
somewhere until your sisters are settled. I would, of course, be responsible
for all the household expenses including those of my sister and Mrs. Darcy."

There was a roaring in her ears as he catalogued the financial arrangements.
She had never been a romantic girl, but this almost mercantile conversation
was oddly distressing.

"I thought to take a small house in, say, Hatfield, for you. I would leave
Anderssen and another man for the outside work and because I will feel
better if there are a couple of strong men to protect a houseful of ladies.
Then, with two or three women for the house, I am sure you could all be
very comfortable." He was beginning to sound a little desperate, and she
realised she had not looked at him for several minutes.

"I am afraid I am not much of a hand at pretty speeches. You must know
that I have come to esteem you as a young lady of compassion and good
sense—just the sort of lady I should wish my sister to become."

Still she could not speak.

"You must not think I would make any…demands upon you right away.
I realise we are almost strangers, and the speed at which we would need to
act will make it difficult for us to become better acquainted before I must
set sail." He smiled wryly. "I have been awake much of the night trying to
decide what to say, and I fear I have not said everything I wished to. I have
been at sea most of my life, and my acquaintance with ladies has been slight.
So I feel woefully unprepared for this conversation, but please believe me
when I say you may always count on my gratitude and trust if you will do
me the great honour of consenting to be my wife."

She stared at him and tried to think. *My sisters, my mother, Mr. Collins,
Longbourn, a shining face smirking, "Lady Catherine is always happy to give
advice," brown eyes in a brown face, a loving embrace for a sister, gratitude,
trust.* Her thoughts whirled. *A little house in Hatfield, calm, order, a chance
to be generous without those wet hands forever and ever, but then Longbourn,
my mother, Jane.* She could see he looked worried and opened her mouth to
ask for a little more time to consider, but before she could speak, the door
to the parlour was flung open.

"Oh, there you are, Lizzy. Mr. Collins wants to talk to you." That round, unctuous face was just behind her mother's shoulder, a look of satisfied possession all over it.

Elizabeth could not bear it, and she realised with a surge of relief that she did not have to. "Mother," she said, "Cousin, you may both congratulate me. Captain Darcy and I are to be married." She saw her intended's face relax into a most becoming smile before they were both overwhelmed by her mother and her complaints.

By the time the house was quiet again, Mr. Bennet had given his consent and absolutely refused to countenance any marriage between Elizabeth and Mr. Collins, Mrs. Bennet had retired to her room in a rage at the destruction of all her plans and only slightly mollified by the details of the settlement, and Mr. Collins had repaired to Lucas Lodge for dinner, mortally offended.

Luckily, the captain had returned to Netherfield before the worst of the uproar. He had kissed her hand, obviously greatly cheered by her acceptance, promising to return on the morrow to make all the arrangements.

Eventually, exhausted by the excitement, Kitty and Lydia's squeals, Jane's concern, and Mary's relief, Elizabeth went to her room, stretched out on her bed, and wept as though her heart would break, muffling her weeping in a pillow for fear that her sister would hear.

Chapter Nine

By the next morning, Elizabeth had scolded herself into a more sanguine state of mind. She could not imagine why she had wept, for the worst had been averted and the future looked much brighter than had seemed possible only hours before. No doubt, it was merely the relief of spirits overwhelmed by worry.

She had always prided herself on her common sense and practicality, and it would be the height of childishness to pine for the sort of declaration found in novels that the Bennet daughters were not supposed to read. No. She was engaged to marry a gentleman she could esteem, look up to even—a gentleman who seemed disposed to appreciate her and to repose his trust in her. That was a great deal more than many young ladies could look forward to.

Breakfast took place in stony silence, and Elizabeth escaped to her father's library as soon as she could. Mr. Bennet had said little to her the previous day and took the opportunity to congratulate her on her conquest. Although he was still weak, Mr. Bennet was obviously cheered by the prospect of his favourite daughter's marriage to an excellent gentleman. "I would welcome the chance to talk to him again," he said, "for he seemed to be a man of good sense and proper feeling." He smiled and patted Elizabeth's hand. "Although I suspect I should regard any man as such who was not Mr. Collins."

Elizabeth was about to protest when the captain was announced. He too appeared much improved in health since the previous day, there being no accompanying sailor to take his arm. He had brought with him a copy of the letter to his attorney in London, detailing the terms of the settlement that had been agreed upon. Although she was somewhat embarrassed, Elizabeth insisted on staying with the gentlemen while matters were decided, it being further agreed that, in view of the need for haste, Mr. Gardiner should be authorised to deal with the attorney in any minor matter that might arise.

As the captain said, "I am due aboard by the twenty-sixth at Portsmouth, so I must leave here not later than the twenty-third, and there is much that must be arranged before then." The date for the wedding was set for two weeks hence on the twenty-first. Meanwhile, the captain was to see about leasing a house in Hatfield. "Should you prefer to be nearer to Meryton, I can easily arrange it; however, I know how difficult it is to set up a new command when you are surrounded by people who knew you as a child. I shall never forget my first ship as captain. I went aboard to find the bosun, the gunner, and the carpenter had all known me as a youngster, and I could never shake the conviction they still saw me as such."

Elizabeth was glad to see that he was prepared to consider her wishes; in all the haste, she could see only too well how easily they could be set aside. "No," she said. "Hatfield would suit admirably—near enough to call for advice should I need it but not so near that I have to take it." Mr. Bennet's laughter had the unfortunate effect of making him cough, and once he was settled, Elizabeth and the captain resolved to take a brief ride in the Netherfield curricle.

It was a bright sunny day, if somewhat cold, and as they trotted along the country lanes, accompanied only by a single groom behind, Elizabeth determined that it was time she came to know the man she had agreed to marry. "It occurs to me, sir, that I do not know your Christian name, and I really cannot marry a man I know only as Captain Darcy."

He looked at her, apparently a little startled, but answered readily enough. "I do not think anyone has called me by my first name since my mother died. It is Fitzwilliam. It will be pleasant to hear it again after all this time."

They rode a little further, Elizabeth pointing out such small sights of interest as the locality afforded. After a few minutes, he spoke again. "I am sure you must have many questions; I have many myself. We have so little time to settle everything that, while question and answer is hardly a polite form of conversation, perhaps we should dispense with the formalities in favour of exchanging as much information as possible."

"Very well," she replied. "May I start by asking what ails you? You seem very well today, but yesterday you needed the support of a strong arm. Were you wounded or is it an illness?"

To her surprise, he laughed. "I think calling it a wound would be stretching the definition. It was merely one of those mishaps common on board ship. The vangs of the b—that is to say, a portion of the rigging parted. The free end swung free and struck me from behind, quite knocking my wits astray." He drew the curricle to a halt and looked down at her. "You must not worry about it. I am well on the way to recovery, and the problem grows less every day. When it happened, I was unconscious for two days and spent a fortnight in my cot with the world reeling about my head. Now, it is merely a question of feeling dizzy occasionally. It is worse when I am tired and, for some reason, worse when I am unsure what I ought to do." He slapped the reins and the horses moved off again. "Perhaps, that is why I continue to suffer on land. I am rarely at a loss at sea."

"And the spectacles?"

"The surgeon's prescription. They are supposed to help the balance, although I have never understood why. They cannot hurt, and so I wear them." They passed the Reverend Carter in his gig at this point and stopped to exchange courtesies and to broach the subject of their wedding. Elizabeth had known him since her childhood and received his heartfelt and kindly blessings, which for some reason made her feel rather shy, although she did her best to respond appropriately.

The parson drove on, and as they left him behind, Elizabeth said, "Now it is your turn to ask a question."

"Very well. Do you think your father strong enough to travel to the Mediterranean with me?"

This was not at all what she had expected, and she hesitated long enough for him to elaborate. "I understood from your mother that the doctor considers that he needs a warmer climate. Although my mission is confidential, my ship is currently refitting at Gibraltar, and it is generally expected to join the Mediterranean fleet. I shall be travelling out on the *Renown*, a 78-gun ship of the line, which must also call in at Gib. The captain is a particular friend of mine and will be happy to take along my guest. There would be room for your father and his man, Starkey can look after all of us, and I happen to know the new Physician to the Fleet is travelling with us, so your father would not lack medical attention."

"But what would he do in Gibraltar? He does not speak the language, and Jessup most assuredly does not."

"You need not concern yourself on that score. There is a large English community at Gibraltar or even, if he wishes to sail further with me, at Malta. All the servants, shops, and lodgings he might want, even books and concerts and such if he is of a mind."

"I am not at all sure he is well enough to travel."

"Might I suggest then that we consult the doctor? Nothing can be decided without his opinion."

They drove a little further in silence. "Have I distressed you with this idea?" he said eventually.

"Oh no!" She turned to him. "It is merely that I am not accustomed to sharing the burden of decision. I seem to have spent the last few months trying to decide what ought to be done from an ever-narrowing selection. It is a great relief to share that burden and yet I feel oddly..." She struggled to find the words.

"Resentful?" he suggested cheerfully. "I know the feeling well. I have sailed on independent cruises, thinking that nothing would be quite as comfortable as having someone with whom to discuss the various decisions I must make, only to find when I returned to the fleet that I deeply resented having someone over me making those decisions."

It was, thought Elizabeth, very cheering to be understood. Even dear Jane would sometimes look blank when Elizabeth tried to explain her feelings. "Very well," she said. "We will ask Doctor Wallace and then, if he thinks it fit, we can ask my father. For I do not trust my papa not to decide he ought to go merely because he thought it might be better for us all at home if he went." She put a hand on his arm. "It is very good of you to think of this. I am quite sure you are discounting a great deal of trouble and inconvenience."

Doctor Wallace, when applied to, seized the idea and recommended it to the hilt. Mrs. Bennet vacillated between declaring that he should not go and that they should all go together. Elizabeth and Jane had considerable difficulty in getting her to understand that four unmarried daughters and a wife could not possibly be accommodated on a battle ship.

Mr. Bennet declared that he was eager to go, had often wished to travel, had been to Ireland as a young man, and had not suffered from the motion at all. However, in view of his condition, it was agreed that the party should leave a day earlier, the day after the wedding, to allow longer for the journey.

A house was found in Hatfield next to the church, with a garden and a space to keep hens. They all travelled out to see it one day, and even Mrs. Bennet had to agree it lacked for nothing. A cook and a housemaid were engaged, and Hill's cousin Maria came from Netherfield to look after the ladies.

It seemed to Elizabeth that the days before the wedding vanished before her eyes. She saw Captain Darcy—Fitzwilliam—only every other day or so, hardly long enough to discover that he liked cake and apples and, despite a life at sea, could not abide the smell of fish. It did not seem nearly long enough to come to understand him more deeply, and she wanted to understand him more as each day passed. She had never met anyone with whom conversation was so easy or whose principles, at least as far as demonstrated in those conversations, so nearly matched her own. As she watched Mr. Collins guzzling his meals, making unnecessary work for the servants, and fawning after Lady Catherine, her heart filled with what she told herself was gratitude and relief. One day, as they walked in the garden with Jane as attendant, Elizabeth asked whether he was sure that he was well enough to go back to sea. "What if you become unwell when climbing around the masts and such?"

His reply was light-hearted enough. "Luckily, we captains are not expected to go aloft, having a ship full of men and junior officers to do that for us." If she was not wholly reassured, she was at least cheered by his promise to find her some books to help her understand his life at sea. She knew she was lucky to be marrying a man so ready to consider her worries and do his best to assuage them and did her best not to repine at the lack of time they would have together. She wondered whether he too regretted their imminent parting but found herself reluctant to ask, although the reason for this reluctance quite escaped her. Her Aunt and Uncle Gardiner and their children came for the ceremony, bringing a delightful dress and bonnet for her trousseau. The inn at Meryton filled with such of the captain's friends who were at liberty, including an immensely tall Captain of Marines and his tiny, doll-like wife, two sea captains so absurdly alike they had to be brothers, a man who looked like a prosperous farmer but turned out to be the new sailing master of the *Achilles,* and a deeply shy young man called Playford, who was to be its new third mate, having recently passed his examination for lieutenant.

The night before the wedding, Mr. Bingley held a dinner in honour of their marriage. All the guests from the Netherfield ball and more were there; Miss Darcy and Mrs. Darcy came down and did their best to express their hopes for their future happiness. Miss Darcy even followed Elizabeth into the ballroom to say how very glad she was that her brother had found her and then found herself being introduced to Lieutenant Playford, who summoned his courage to solicit his captain's sister as a dancing partner.

Elizabeth danced with Mr. Bingley, she danced with Jack Catteral whom she had known since childhood, and finally she danced with her intended. She was so proud of him, so tall, handsome, composed, active and successful in his profession and in scenes of life so far from anything she had ever known. He was attentive and considerate to her and patient with her mother and Mr. Collins, who could not politely be missed from the invitation.

Over supper, as her friends and acquaintances interrupted to congratulate them, he told her something of his travels, of Africa and the Orient, of strange people and animals, of friends and enemies made and lost. She saw him fully as a man of consequence and power and regretted ever more deeply that he must leave so soon after she had come to know him.

They closed the ball together, and every time they touched hands, her heart warmed. He had a slight smile on his face as they danced, and she hoped that he was feeling as happy as she was. They hardly spoke; it did not seem necessary. All had been decided, and all that remained was the ceremony; she refused to consider the parting that would follow.

As he bade her farewell at the door of Netherfield, he kissed her hand and then bent and kissed her cheek. She felt his warm breath and the pressure of his lips and could not restrain a small sigh of happiness. As the coach took them back to Longbourn, she relived their dances and that moment at the door and did not feel the cold at all.

Chapter Ten

That night, Elizabeth got in bed with Jane, as she so often had as a child, and they whispered the night away. In all the bustle and preparations, she had almost forgotten how much she would miss her elder sister, and it took Jane some time and considerable effort to reassure Elizabeth that she did not resent being left behind at Longbourn. "I know Mama can be difficult," said Jane. "But now that Aunt and Uncle Gardiner are to take Lydia back to London, I am sure Kitty, Mary, and I will be able to live in something like rational peace."

"And Kitty or Mary can always come and stay with me for a while," replied Elizabeth. "I fear we have neglected them somewhat, and Mary in particular seems never to have had a confidential friend."

"We shall do better, shall we not?"

"Yes." She looked at Jane slyly. "And now there is no need for hurry, perhaps you and Mr. Bingley will have time to become properly acquainted." Even though they had only candlelight, Elizabeth could see her sister blush deeply before Jane brought the conversation to a halt by attacking her sister with a pillow.

Mrs. Bennet woke them at a ridiculously early hour and then confused them both with a murmured lecture on the duties of marriage, a lecture that required a further discussion with Mrs. Gardiner to become intelligible. Considerably relieved, for she had known nothing for certain before, and her imaginings had all been based on farm animals, Elizabeth suffered her mother to weep over her while she dressed and ate what little breakfast she could manage.

It had been intended that her Uncle Gardiner would give her away, as the trip to the church was considered too arduous for her father. However, about an hour before the service was due to start, an elderly sedan chair arrived—carried by Captain Darcy's two men—that had apparently been found in the Netherfield stables. It smelt a little of smoke due to the attempts to air it through but was completely dry, and Mr. Bennet announced his intention of going to church, and nothing anybody could say would dissuade him.

So Elizabeth walked down the aisle on her father's arm, the pews filled with a gay company of family, friends, and dress uniforms. The captain stood waiting for her, gallant in navy blue, the Nile medal on a ribbon in his buttonhole, gold lace and epaulettes gleaming. She hardly heard the service, except for his deep voice repeating the vows. Everything else was drowned out by the beat of her heart, a sense that time and place were not entirely real and that she might wake at any moment and find herself once more in bed with Jane.

Afterwards, it was the smells she remembered: the flowers in her bouquet and bonnet, the smoke from the candles, the charcoal from the brazier someone had placed in the family pew for her father, and when the captain bent to kiss her cheek again, the soap he had shaved with.

When they left the church, all the naval guests and their servants had formed up to make an arch of their swords and they bent their heads and ran laughing through them to the coach that was to take them back to Longbourn, only to find that the horses had been removed and her father's tenants had taken the traces to pull them home in a shower of dried flower petals and good wishes.

The wedding breakfast was scarcely more intelligible to her. Her mother had done her proud, and there was ample food and drink, including real French champagne, a wedding gift from Mr. Bingley. Perhaps it was the champagne, for despite the fact that there were so many strangers present, there was no awkwardness or polite silences. The two Captains Hanson made themselves particularly agreeable and were invited to stay for a few days longer to go hunting with Robert Lucas and his friends. Elizabeth passed amongst the guests on her new husband's arm, feeling his warm, living strength beneath her hand, and she could not remember afterwards who had spoken to her and what they had said, save that they were happy for her and confident in his care for her.

The only thing lacking for perfection was her father's presence; exhausted by the ceremony despite the accommodations made for him, he soon retired to his bed. She went to see him in his chamber, wrapped in his nightshirt and shawls. At his command, she bent over and he kissed her forehead. "I am so very happy for you, child," he said softly. "I have worried for many years that you might not find a gentleman who would appreciate you. If anything happens to me on this voyage, I can at least be satisfied that you are safe."

"Sir," she replied. "I hope to see you return to us restored in health before very long." He opened his mouth to object, but she laid a gentle finger on his lips. "And you may safely leave Mama and the girls to Jane and me—with a little help from Uncle Gardiner." He smiled at this, and she left him preparing to sleep.

There were tears when it was time for her to leave. Longbourn would never again be her home; she would visit it and be welcome, but it was no longer hers, and she could not help but weep for that a little. However, as the coach left Meryton, she wiped her eyes and smiled at her husband. "There," she said. "I am done." He handed her his handkerchief, a piece of silk the size of a small sail, and she dried her eyes. "It seems you are forever coming to my rescue. You must not think I am normally such a watering pot," she said, returning it.

"I think you a lady of courage and feeling," he replied firmly. "Such a new life, on such short notice is enough to make anyone weep. I am feeling more than a little overwhelmed myself. Tell me, did you sleep last night?"

"Not a wink."

"Nor I. I hope I shall be a good husband. For all that I shall be at sea, I would wish to do my best for you," he said.

"I have no fear on that score," she replied.

He smiled at that and came over to sit on her side of the coach, taking her hand. "Have I told you today how beautiful you look?"

"Yes; however, it is a sentiment that bears repetition."

He took her hand and kissed it gently. "I could hardly believe my good fortune when I saw you walk into the church."

"You must credit my Aunt Gardiner for that, for it was her choice of gown and bonnet."

"In the navy, we call that 'fishing for compliments,' for you know quite well that, becoming as they were, I do not refer to your gown or your bonnet." He laughed. "Are you blushing, my...my dear? And I thought you such a strong-minded young lady."

"If you can find a young lady who does not blush at such things, then I fear you have not found a lady at all," she replied and then blushed more deeply.

He raised an arm and tucked her into his side with a murmured, "May I?" and they sat in companionable silence while the coach rocked through the gathering darkness to their new home. Miss Darcy and her mother were staying at Netherfield for the night and no one was at the Hatfield house save for the servants, but it was warm and welcoming, the scent of lavender and beeswax showing that time and care had been taken to make it ready.

In the parlour, they sat down to tea and business. "I am afraid there is much we must discuss before I leave," he said, spreading papers on the tea table. "I have opened accounts for you at two banks, and the dividends from your settlement will be paid half into each. The County Bank failed last month so it is best to divide one's risk. I have placed money in both for housekeeping and your use until the dividends fall due next month and shall continue to deposit money for the household bills and your expenses."

She murmured her thanks, but he waved them away. "I have arranged for a good man to keep the garden. His name is Puttnam, and he will arrive tomorrow or the day after. He lost a foot, poor fellow, but he was a market gardener before he took the bounty, so he should do well for you. Anderssen has been my cox'n these many years and can be trusted absolutely. His language may be a little coarse, but he is discreet and honest. Here is his sick ticket. He picked up a nasty splinter wound and should not be at sea. He will need the ticket if the Press come calling. A prime seaman like him is worth his weight in gold."

Business took up another hour. As for why there was no horse and carriage: "I have arranged a contract with the King's Head to hire you a carriage and driver whenever you wish to go to Longbourn. I did not think there would be enough use to warrant buying an equipage outright, although if there is, you can always make your own arrangements." What to do about letters: "Grace will know my direction, and if you hand your letters to him, he will know how to see I get them. Ship-to-ship is much more reliable that the post, although if you do write, please ensure you date and number your letters so I can see whether any have gone astray." News about Mr. Bennet: "I shall write here in the first instance, and you can decide what and how much to pass on to Longbourn."

Most distressing, however, were the details of what should happen if he were killed at sea. "This is my will. You may read it when I am gone. Suffice it to say that I would wish you to look after my sister until she is settled. I put no other obligation upon you. You will receive any arrears of pay, my books, and anything else you wish to keep. I have a small inheritance from my godfather, Judge Darcy, which is largely untouched, and this will go to Georgiana but not before she is five-and-twenty. I do not want any more fortune-hunting parsons sniffing round her."

When at last it was all done, they looked round the house together. She was touched to find her father had sent all her favourite books from his library, with some she did not recognise including *The Midshipman's Remembrancer—Being a Manual of Seamanship, Navigation and Conduct at Sea* and one or two others. She realised the latter were of the captain's providing in fulfilment of a promise she herself had quite forgotten. There was a brand-new cabinet piano for Georgiana's use, and all the bedrooms were newly painted, with fresh hangings on the beds.

They dined together, simply but well, still talking of all that needed to be said between them. Elizabeth was a little concerned that the captain's older brother, Mr. Darcy, might attempt to regain custody of his sister. "I cannot think it at all likely," replied her husband. "Not only is he idle in the last degree, but I have a temporary injunction remitting her to my custody while the issue is still at law, a matter I do not expect to be settled for many months, if not years. If worst comes to worst, Grace will get you both passage to the Mediterranean on a suitable ship, and my brother and that sot of a parson of his can whistle for her money."

"You place a great deal of trust in me, sir."

He smiled and placed a hand over hers. "I do. I suppose many years at sea have accustomed me to assessing at speed the character of those I meet. I have known you to be a person of intelligence and decision since first we met. There are many things in this life I am uncertain of; you are not numbered amongst them."

It was time to retire. The information from her mother and Mrs. Gardiner was running through her mind. He had said he would make no demands, but perhaps she might offer? No, that would be beyond bold, and even if she had not feared to look in some fashion unladylike or even wanton, how did one say it? She undressed and got into her second-best nightgown, for somehow she had never retrieved the one Jane had borrowed. Maria came in, brushed her hair, and removed the warming pan. Then she giggled, wished her mistress a goodnight, and vanished.

Elizabeth could hear him moving in the dressing room next door. There was a bang, the sound of something metal hitting the floor, and a muffled something that was probably an oath. She dared not get out of bed, so she called out, "Is everything all right?" Gathering her courage, she added, "Fitzwilliam?"

He appeared in the doorway in his dressing gown and nightshirt, gripping the side of the door. "I'm sorry if I disturbed you. I am afraid it's the da... dashed dizziness again. I knocked my purse onto the floor and when I bent down to pick it up—there it was. My own fault for not sleeping properly last night."

"Where will you sleep?"

He came into the room and gingerly made his way to the bed. "You must not think I have come to make a nuisance of myself, but it occurs to me that it would be as well if I spent the night here. It would not do for word to get out that I did not, as it might raise suspicions about the marriage that my brother's lawyers could exploit." She must have looked alarmed or something, for he quickly added, "I can easily sleep in that armchair. One thing about a life at sea is that it teaches one to sleep almost anywhere."

She looked at his face. He appeared sincere, and why should she doubt his word now? He had never been anything but kind and considerate of her feelings. He closed his eyes and held on to the covers, his knuckles whitening. She made up her mind. "This is a great nonsense, sir. We are married, and the very least I can do is offer you a bed in your own home." She held up one side of the covers and then hopped out of bed, went round the other side, helped him out of his dressing gown and then into bed.

When she climbed back in, she found him lying on his back, his eyes still tight shut. She took his hand in hers and squeezed it.

"You are being very kind," he said softly.

"It is no more than you deserve," she replied. "How is your head?"

"No worse than before. I can usually sleep it off."

"Then you should do so now. Goodnight, Fitzwilliam."

He raised the hand he held to his lips. "Goodnight, my dear."

Somewhat to her surprise, they were both asleep in minutes.

Chapter Eleven

S he had never before shared a bed with anyone quite so large, and several times in the night, she turned over and bumped into an unexpected shoulder or knee. Once she awoke with a large, heavy arm round her waist and lay awake for a moment wondering whether he had awakened too and whether this were a preparatory move before...but she must have been more tired that she had thought, for she fell asleep again before she could decide whether or not she would welcome his attentions. When she awakened the next morning, she was alone.

She sat up, suddenly afraid he might have left before bidding her goodbye, until the sound of someone singing softly in the dressing room reassured her.

Farewell and adieu to you Spanish ladies
Farewell and adieu to you ladies of Spain
For we've received orders to sail for old England
But we hope in a short time to see you again.

He had a pleasant, tuneful voice, and she lay in bed for a few minutes listening to it until a glance at the curtained windows showed it was getting light, so she hurried to wash and dress, anxious to make the best of what little time they had left. She passed Starkey on the landing with her husband's shaving water and stopped to have a word with him, only to find that she could think of nothing to say that would not sound foolish. It was obvious, however, that the man was no fool, for he ducked his head to her and said softly, "Never you mind, missus, I'll look after 'im." Then he bolted before she could express her thanks.

They had breakfast in the little dining room, and she was startled to see what a six-foot sea captain considered a proper breakfast. Her own little plate was quite dwarfed by the beefsteak, eggs, bacon, and toast he devoured. When he reached for his sixth slice, he caught her looking at him and grinned. "Once you've lived on ship's biscuit, you can never get enough soft tack," he said, and she made a mental note to always have new bread in the house when he came home.

The clock in the hall, a gift from her Aunt Phillips, chimed eight. The coach would be arriving soon. "Fitzwilliam, are you sure you are well enough to go to sea? After last night, I wonder whether you should not be given a sick ticket as well. Can you not leave your ship with another captain until you are quite recovered?"

He drained his coffee cup and took her hand over the breakfast things. "I wish I could. It is difficult to explain because my mission is confidential." He bit his lower lip and then said, "This is strictly *entre nous,* you understand?" She nodded. "I am ordered to make contact with…certain forces on land that might change their allegiance and join with us against the Corsican. These people know me personally and are not disposed to deal with anyone else. It is not a question of the great powers, merely of smaller principalities and such that might be persuaded to offer us aid. You can have no idea how much wood and water a ship requires, and any assistance I can obtain will be extremely useful.

"Frankly, I consider the whole business a great nonsense, and if anything comes of it, I shall be amazed. However, the attempt must be made, and it is up to me to make it."

"Is it dangerous?"

"There is little enough in this war that is not," he replied and then raised his head at the sound of a carriage stopping in the street outside. "I think it is time." Starkey came in with his greatcoat and hat, and she flung a shawl about her shoulders and followed him into the street.

Her father was sitting in the carriage, swathed in shawls and rugs. His man Jessup, who was scarcely any younger than his master, sat on the box looking glum.

Elizabeth climbed into the coach to bid her father farewell and extract a promise to write often and at length about his journey. There was a net of books beside him on the carriage wall, and a bag of all his various medicines under the care of Lieutenant Playford, who was to ride down with them. She could think of nothing more she could do for his comfort since they were to pick up newly warmed bricks at the inn, so they exchanged kisses and goodbyes and did their best not to think this might be their last meeting. Surprisingly, it was not difficult to do so. Mr. Bennet looked frail, but he was not coughing, and his face shone with all the excitement of a boy on an adventure.

Then it was time to say goodbye to *him*. When she climbed out of the coach, she saw him embracing his sister who was weeping and trying hard not to. Their eyes met over her fair head, and he smiled and bent down to kiss his sister. "Now then, my dear," he said gently. "You must let me say goodbye to my wife."

Freed from his sister's embrace, he came over to stand by her. "It seems so unfair that I have to leave so soon," he said.

"But if you had not had to leave so soon, we might never have...I do not want you to go." She had not meant to say that.

"Neither do I, but I must." He bowed low and kissed her hand. Then when he straightened, his breath hitched and, before she knew what was happening, she was in his arms. "I would give anything," he muttered and kissed her.

Their noses bumped and she could feel the buttons on his greatcoat pressing into her, then he turned his head slightly and it was warm and wet and shockingly intimate. She clung to his shoulders, opened her mouth to him, and suddenly it felt as though she had lived all her life behind thick glass walls. Everything was nearer, brighter, louder and more alive. He tightened his grip, his tongue touched hers, and her throat filled with something unbearable but beautiful.

Then one of the horses stamped its foot and snorted, and the moment was over. They let go of one another, and it felt like something breaking. He kissed her briefly on the cheek and turned to do the same to his sister. As he turned to climb into the coach, she remembered. "Wait a moment," she called and ran back into the house and returned a moment later with a soft bundle she thrust into his hands. "It is a comforter. I knitted it for you."

Her father heard her, and from within the coach she could hear him laugh. "You knitted it? Must be a Job's comforter." And she knew her husband would be regaled with stories of her various failures in the womanly arts on his journey to Portsmouth. He, however, thanked her warmly and promised to wear it at sea.

And then there could be no more delay. He climbed into the carriage next to her father, and it drove off down the street, Georgiana and Elizabeth waving their handkerchiefs until the carriage turned the corner and was gone.

The house felt empty without him, but there was much to do, and if she did not keep them both busy, the pair of them would sit down and cry like babies. So she dried her eyes, shook herself, and took her new sister on a tour of their new home.

Mrs. Darcy, who had scuttled indoors the moment she and Georgiana had arrived, had already possessed herself of the best of the two remaining bedrooms and had commandeered Maria to open the trunks that had been delivered the previous day. Elizabeth had intended the room for Georgiana, but that young lady was delighted with the remaining room and its view over the garden, so Elizabeth let matters lie.

The piano nearly overset Georgiana's composure, but she managed to master herself and finish the tour. She pronounced it the prettiest cottage ever, and Elizabeth wondered anew about Pemberley. What sort of a place must it be if Miss Darcy thought this substantial house merely a cottage?

Meanwhile, there was much to be done. Mrs. Manning, the cook, wished to discuss the menus for the week, Anderssen announced that the roof of the room over the stables, where he and Puttnam were to sleep, leaked, and Mrs. Darcy wanted something done about the smell of pigs and so on and so on. Elizabeth had never been in sole charge of a household before and found the whole business much more complicated that she had thought. Hill and Cook had known their jobs perfectly well without direction and, in any case, Jane and her mother were there to do their part. Now she had to do it all herself, and for a moment she was daunted.

But only for a moment. Mrs. Manning was requested to ragout the remains of last night's joint, Anderssen was given half a crown to buy pitch and nails, and Mrs. Darcy was informed that the pigs in the next-door garden were an unfortunate fact of life and would have to be borne. Once those matters were dealt with, Elizabeth settled down to the job of working out how to run a household.

Anderssen was of enormous assistance. It seemed that the man could turn his hand to anything, from mending the roof to rehanging a door. Within the week, every unsteady shelf, rattling window, and squeaking hinge had been dealt with. Although he was never impolite, he did not talk much, and when he did, the loss of his front teeth made much of what he said unintelligible, but he was willing and blessedly competent, and Elizabeth never had to worry about the house.

Puttnam, when he arrived, was much more loquacious and soon became something of a local curiosity, for instead of the traditional peg, he had replaced his missing foot with a carved wooden one with an ingenious hinge and could be heard stumping down the street with alternative footsteps of hobnails and teak. He tutted over the garden and the hen run, doubted they would ever produce much, prophesied cabbage root fly, black spot, yellow jackets, ravenous pigeons, and moles, then within three days had dug it all over and was promising that by summer they would never have to buy a vegetable again.

The days were busy, but Elizabeth found the nights uncomfortably long and quiet. Lydia and Kitty were frequently exasperating, but at least they made a usually cheerful noise about the place. Many nights found Elizabeth lying awake in her enormous bed, wondering how she came to be there, a married woman without a husband, when only weeks before she had been single and afraid.

She could not help worrying until a letter came from Portsmouth. Her father, although tired, had arrived safe and sound. Since the wind was against them, they were putting up at a quiet hotel used by naval wives and families visiting the port. "I have come to believe that every travelling party should contain a naval officer," he wrote. "Difficulties are sorted, landlords quelled, and post boys cowed. I do not think I ever have known a less harassing journey." Her husband was apparently busy arranging for the voyage, for there was but a brief note from him, assuring them of the whole party's health and well being. A note at the bottom added that he was wearing her comforter beneath his coat.

As the house gradually settled into its daily routine, callers began to appear. Mrs. Bennet and her sisters came over from Longbourn, Mrs. Bennet full of complaints about the loss of Mr. Bennet and Lydia and especially about her brother Gardiner's tyranny with the housekeeping money. Elizabeth did her best to represent the need for economy without revealing she knew the funds were really under Jane's control. As her mother and younger sisters ranged about the house exclaiming and comparing, Elizabeth and Jane managed a few minutes of mutual condolence on the difficulties of running a house alone.

The day after her family visited, Lieutenant Grace and his wife came to call. While they all drank tea in the parlour, she asked him where he had met her husband, and she was rewarded by a stream of reminiscence. "We were shipmates aboard the old *Lincoln*," he said. "I was second, and he was a master's mate. He could not have been more than fifteen or sixteen, but I was right glad to have him aboard. She were a nasty old ship, the *Lincoln*. When she wasn't hogging, she was sagging and crank nor you wouldn't believe!"

"Lemuel," said his wife reprovingly, and he looked up guiltily.

"Am I talking too much? Always did talk too much." Elizabeth hurried to assure him that she very much wanted to hear, and he continued. "Well, she was a bad-tempered sort of ship—needed a lot of nursing or she'd turn on you. The captain was drinking himself to death, and the premier was a bl...a fool. Your husband and I kept that old tub afloat on the Toulon blockade until she was dismasted in a storm. We had far too many landsmen aboard and not near enough right seamen, but we managed to get her back to port." He laughed a little bitterly. "The surveyor took one good look and condemned her out of hand. I spent the next four years on the beach on half pay. You don't get fat on four guineas a month and find yourself, let me tell you. Any road, for all he were nobbut a lad, your husband were a grand help. I'd never have done it without him." He took a big gulp of his tea, and the next few minutes were spent with his wife patting him on the back and chiding him for drinking it too hot.

When they finally settled back in their chairs, Georgiana, who had been listening with shining eyes, asked the lieutenant how old he had been when he went to sea.

"Oh, I were twelve and wild to go to sea, like my cousin Frank. There were six of us at home and my mother at her wits' end to know what to do with us all."

"My brother was only nine, and that seems terribly young."

"It is, miss," he replied. "But your brother was lucky with his captain. He was on the *Illustrious*, a second rate." Seeing her puzzlement, he added, "A powerful big ship. There'd be over a score of young gentlemen aboard, and Captain Hanning-Ward was always very particular about the way they was taught. Shipped his own cousin as schoolmaster and made sure they didn't just learn navigation like usual. Always said he expected his young gentlemen to learn to write a decent letter or report and know what was going on in the world. That's why they call him "Professor"—'cause there are a lot of captains who leave the mids to bring themselves up, and he wasn't having any of that."

This was at least a little consolation, but that night as she lay in bed, Elizabeth could not help but imagine her husband as a very small boy, surrounded by other larger boys, sitting at a long table, and practising the use of logarithms under the watchful eye of the captain's cousin.

Chapter Twelve

Christmas was a difficult time for Elizabeth, the first she had ever spent away from Longbourn, and since her Aunt and Uncle Gardiner and their children were staying, there was no room for Elizabeth and her new relations. Instead, they went to Longbourn for Christmas Day and returned that evening, finding the house quiet and rather dull after the bustle at her mother's house. There was no letter from her husband or her father until the end of the year when one arrived announcing their safe arrival in Gibraltar.

It was her husband who had written, and the letter took the shape of a short journal, detailing their days at sea and how her father was managing the naval life. It began rather formally, "Dear Madam," but continued in a more conversational tone.

"It was horribly rough in the Chops of the Channel," he wrote. *"And your father very wisely stayed in his cot. I was afraid that the conditions might be too much for him, but Doctor James, who travels with us, was very kind, and by the time conditions calmed, he was much better. The cough continues, but the doctor approves the remedies Wallace sent with him and feels sure the warmer weather will help."*

Several days later, he added that her father had just won ten shillings off the captain of the *Renown* at whist, and would Elizabeth please forward Johnson's *Life of Savage* and his Greek *Herodotus*. *"I left him having a ferociously learned discussion with the Captain of Marines, and I suspect he means to stun him with chapter and verse if they ever meet again. He would, no doubt, write himself save that he cannot get the trick of managing a pen at sea. The second time it slid across the page and scored out everything he had written, he gave up and vowed he will not write another line until he stands on dry land."*

Additionally, and delightfully, it appeared that Captain Darcy was something of an artist. There was a charming pen and ink drawing of her father asleep in something between a chair and a hammock and another of Jessup looking at a ship's biscuit with an expression of alarm.

There were occasional comments about the ship and its manoeuvres, and Elizabeth did her best to decipher them with the aid of the *Remembrancer* and, when that failed, Lieutenant Grace. Given the truly astonishing number of ropes, sails, and other equipment, she knew she would probably never understand it all, but she resolved to make the effort. After a little persuading, Anderssen even came indoors and taught her some of the common knots and hitches. He still said very little but sat patiently doing the knots over and over again until she had mastered them. She was particularly proud of something called a "Double Matthew Walker," which was ornamental in the highest degree, so she tied them in every piece of cord in the house.

Although she was a little concerned that her letter in reply to her husband might seem dull to him, engaged as he was in a public and active life, Lieutenant Grace reassured her. "Oh no, ma'am, quite the opposite. There's nothing better than a letter that lets you see what life is like at home and shows you that you haven't been forgotten. Might make a man feel homesick, but that's better than being forgotten."

So she told him everything, acquiring the habit of sitting down at the end of each day to note down for him the daily round. She was, however, careful to begin her letter *"My Dear Fitzwilliam,"* and hoped that in doing so she might tempt him into a warmer address.

She told him of the way the vicar's son had fallen in love with Georgiana, utterly undeterred by the fact that he was only six years of age. *"He informed her that he is doing his best to grow up as quickly as possible so that they can get married. She was, I thought, very kind and did not point out the logical flaw in the proposal."*

She told him about the slates that came off the roof and had to be replaced by Anderssen using ladders and a great deal of rope. *"Lieutenant Grace came to assist, and I am persuaded they both enjoyed themselves immensely, climbing up and down and hauling things and calling Puttnam a 'lubber' when he let go."*

She told him about the housemaid who was caught stealing feathers from

Mrs. Darcy's bed and had to be dismissed and replaced with one of the Reverend Carter's protégées. *"She is a thin, shy, wispy girl who answers to the scarcely believable name of 'Hepszibah.' I was not sure she was up to the work, but over the last fortnight, one might swear she was visibly swelling under the twin influences of good food and kindness. She still says hardly anything, but this morning I rather think I heard her singing as she worked."*

She did not tell him about the time she found herself under the disagreeable necessity of taking Mrs. Darcy to task for monopolising Maria; with three ladies to take care of, it was not fair to demand so much of the girl's attention. She had tried to be patient, for a very little thought had shown her that the lady could have been no older than Georgiana when she married, and Elizabeth knew that life with her husband's brother had not been pleasant. However, with only three of them in the house, she also knew that, unless some basic courtesies were agreed upon, life might soon become exceedingly difficult.

She was somewhat surprised by Mrs. Darcy's reaction. The lady first flinched and then, when no further remonstration occurred, she ventured a timid protest. Then, when her protest was kindly but firmly rebuffed, she sulked for an hour and then settled down apparently quite happy under the new regime. Thinking it over in bed that night, Elizabeth realised that Mrs. Darcy was rather like Kitty and, indeed, like Amelia Goulding and several other young ladies and gentlemen of her acquaintance. She needed to be told what was expected of her and, so long as the discipline was firm, she would do as she was told. She wondered uncomfortably what it said of a middle-aged gentleman like her husband's father that he should have chosen such a wife.

However little she might say of her new sister's mother, she thought her husband might like to hear about his sister, especially considering he had known so little of her growing up. *"I have taken the liberty of hiring masters for her,"* she wrote. *"She says almost nothing about her life at Pemberley, but it appears that her education was somewhat neglected.*

"It was a little difficult to find anyone in so small a place as Hatfield, but there is an émigré gentleman who teaches her French and Italian, an excellent lady who teaches drawing and water colours, and a gentleman who visits once a fortnight to improve her piano playing. I am so little of a musician that I thought she required no teaching in that respect, but she was so earnest in her

desire to learn, I thought it as well to accede. He comes from St. Albans in a gig and is sinfully expensive, but Georgiana says she has and continues to learn much, so for the time being, the lessons continue."

It was almost a wrench to let the letter go; however, one day the lieutenant came to inform her that a suitable ship would be sailing shortly, so she finished it hurriedly with her assurances of the household's health and well being, asked him whether he was still troubled with the dizziness, and told him that she prayed for his safe return. Then she added the letter to the parcel of books her father had requested and handed them over with a slightly shamefaced kiss to the address.

A letter from him arrived less than a week later, although she did not receive it until she returned from an evening party at the rectory. She thought for a moment that it might be his reply before realising it must have been sent long before her own missive could arrive. Georgiana and her mother were already making their way up to bed, so she did not mention the letter and resolved to read it alone. She went into the parlour, stirred the fire into life, and lit the lamp from its flames.

It was still addressed, *"Dear Madam,"* and she might have been troubled by that, had she not told herself firmly that she was very probably the first lady he had corresponded with since his mother died and determined not to worry until he had received her last. The letter was headed "Aboard *HMS Achilles,"* and it began by assuring her of her father's continuing improvement and his determination to stay on the ship as far as Malta.

Someone told him that it can take several days to regain one's 'sea legs.' So he has remained aboard, mostly playing chess with the purser and reading such books as the ship affords. This time he would like you to send Suetonius, Plutarch's Lives, and Tristram Shandy. The weather here is considerably warmer that it will be in England, although it is still far from hot. I shall ensure he is provided with suitable warm weather clothing before I set him ashore.

I arrived here to find that the dockyard have still not finished the fitting out. It appears that my new first lieutenant is an amiable young man, entirely lacking in energy or authority. When I add that he is nephew to Admiral Pascoe, I have said everything that need be said. I have spent the last few days harrying and hounding the world and his wife in an effort to get to sea in anything like good order.

To make matters worse, the port admiral has drafted forty of my men into the

"Endymion" which left last week and replaced them with the scouring of the prisons. 'King's Hard Bargains,' we call them, and a harder set I have never seen. You may tell Anderssen that my new coxswain is half the man he is and needs twice the telling.

Luckily, Cavendish the Second and Playford know what they are about, and the new master is really excellent. With their help, I hope to get to sea tomorrow so that I can start turning this ragbag into a decent crew.

The rest of the letter was a description of the harbour at Malta, and the drawing this time was of her father and Jessup in wide-brimmed straw hats, sitting on coils of rope. He signed off with his best wishes for her continued health and happiness and his love to his sister.

She thought the letter finished there, but when she turned the page over, almost automatically, not expecting anything further, she found an additional paragraph, the handwriting hurried.

"It is difficult to believe how much difference it makes to a man to have some-one at home to whom he can write. In the past, I have envied shipmates who receive letters and, most of all, have envied their connection with home and family and England. I say this not to place upon you the burden of a lengthy correspondence if you are not of a mind, but merely to beg the favour of an oc-casional line from you" (the words *"and Georgiana"* had been added at this point) *"so that I might sleep easy in the knowledge that you are safe and well."* It was signed merely *FD.*

She read and re-read that paragraph, before turning to the rest of the letter. Then, when she had finished it, she turned to the back and read it again, and as she did so, she thought she might weep. She was hunting round for a handkerchief, determined to go to bed at last, when there was a tap on the parlour door, and to her astonishment, Puttnam came in.

"Begging your pardon, ma'am," he said. "But Anderssen and me thought you ought to know. There's some shady coves been hanging around all day, town-bred by the looks of 'em. One of 'em was in the Eagle asking about the young lady." He hitched his head towards the bedrooms upstairs. "And one of 'em 'as been 'anging around in the lane out back."

Chapter Thirteen

Elizabeth sat down heavily. "We just walked back from the rectory in the dark," she said weakly.

"Never you mind about that, ma'am. We knew the vicar'd send his man with you with a light, and me and Anderssen have been walking up and down the lane with a dark lantern, making out we thought someone was after the 'ens. 'Oo ever were out there hooked it sharpish." He saw her looking at him and added, "Ran away."

Elizabeth did her best to cudgel her brains into life. "And they were asking for Miss Darcy by name?"

"Yes'm and they described her to a T. They've ordered a chaise to be ready as soon as they call for it. The captain, well, 'e warned Anderssen there might be trouble from 'is brother from up North. We reckon—Anderssen and me—that they're mebbe sent by him to take her back."

"Do you know how many of them there are?"

"We think there's only two," he replied, "a bandy-legged cove with a catskin waistcoat and a big, nasty-looking piece o' work in corduroy breeches—prize-fighting sort. O' course there's mebbe more we 'aven't seen."

"Do you think they will try to get into the house?" She looked around, suddenly conscious of the quiet and the nearby door to the street.

He was reassuring. "Nah, me and Anderssen put them shutters up and the locks on the door, like the captain told us, and they couldn't get in without making a fu…a lot of noise. We was thinking, Anderssen and me, that if you was to bunk in with one of the other ladies, he could keep watch from the kitchen and I'd keep a watch from your room, and if they did try anything in the night, we'd wake the 'ole town up."

She sat in silence for a while, thinking hard. It was not as though these mysterious newcomers had done anything yet, and even if they did, who was to stop them? She looked up at Puttnam. "Who is the town constable?" she said.

"Bless you, ma'am," he replied. "Poor old Jenkins? I reckon you could take him in a fight, begging your pardon. We did wonder about the lobsters in Meryton, but they're not even marines. I don't suppose the captain left a pistol in the house?"

She shook her head, beyond being shocked at the suggestion. "Perhaps Lieutenant Grace?" she suggested. She got to her feet in sudden decision. "I shall sleep with Miss Darcy tonight," she said. "Please fetch me a large knife from the kitchen, just in case, and if you and Anderssen would keep watch tonight, we can decide what to do in the morning."

Georgiana was sleepily surprised to see her but seemed to accept the idea that Elizabeth had had a bad dream and soon went back to sleep. She never noticed the boning knife Elizabeth hid under her pillow.

It was raining heavily the next day with a cold, gusting wind that sent leaves and rubbish swirling. Hardly anyone was voluntarily about in the streets, which made it easier to spot bandy-legs and prize-fighter. A third man joined them during the day, swathed to the eyebrows in an old-fashioned, caped driving coat, although he spent most of his time drinking in the King's Head.

About half past ten in the morning, three ladies accompanied by a manservant came out of the house and hurried up the street to another house, some fifty yards away. The ladies were almost hidden in their bonnets and overcoats and could only be distinguished by the colours of their coats: brown, green, and blue. Halfway there, the lady in the dark blue surtout lost her bonnet to a gust of wind which released a mass of dark golden hair. She turned to chase after it, and green coat called out to "Georgiana" to be careful. Once the bonnet was retrieved, all three ladies linked arms and approached the other house. They knocked and were admitted by a maid.

Several hours later, brown coat and green coat and the manservant went back to their own house. It had come on to rain even harder, and the ladies were huddled under an umbrella that threatened to escape their grasp at any time. Once they made their front door, two men came out and secured all the shutters.

Time passed. It started to grow dark, and the few passers-by there had been disappeared. Thunder rolled.

Suddenly, the door to the second house was flung open and blue surtout came out. A voice from inside called, "Oh, do come back, Miss Darcy! My husband will be here to take you home in a few minutes," before the wind blew the door shut again. The coat headed off down the road and looked up. The three strangers were converging on its wearer and were already alarmingly close. She gave a cry of alarm and turned back, but seeing the closed door she had just left, she darted up a small lane between two houses instead.

The three scoundrels pounded after her, their coat tails blowing in the wind. They were just in time to see their quarry turning to the right at the top of the lane, so they headed after her, prize-fighter pulling an old sack from his pocket as they ran. They were halfway up when they were suddenly blinded by a wash of light.

Two men stood at the end of the lane, dark lanterns now opened and fully lit at their feet, holding stout cudgels that they smacked into their palms with looks not so much of menace as of satisfaction. Despite the fact that one of them had a false foot, they were both large and alarmingly calm. The three confederates looked to turn back, only to find that the other end was also blocked, this time by two large men in blacksmiths' aprons with hammers in their hands.

There was a moment's silence before prize-fighter and bandy-legs decided to make a fight of it. They rushed towards the first two men while driving coat tried to make a run for it.

Peeping round the end of the house, Elizabeth could see very little, especially when one of the lanterns was kicked over, but she heard sounds of a struggle, a lot of very bad language, and then silence. She tugged the blue coat closer to herself for comfort.

Lieutenant Grace came out of the shadows and uncocked the pistol Elizabeth had not even known he was carrying. Puttnam and Anderssen shook hands with the blacksmith and his son, and a small amount of money changed hands, despite protestations that it had been a pleasure. "To drink the captain and his lady's health" was the finally successful argument. The lieutenant hurried Elizabeth back indoors where his wife was waiting, pale with fright. They both plied Elizabeth with currant wine, which she secretly thought very unpleasant, and compliments on her bravery.

"I admire your strategy, m'dear," he said, as he walked her back to her own front door. "The true Nelson touch."

That night, in her journal-cum-letter to her husband, she mentioned the weather and tea with the lieutenant and his wife, but nothing else. She had no desire to burden him with her thoughts and fears, for the day had been terrifying in the extreme. Georgiana was not nearly so discreet in her letter, admiration and gratitude spilling over the page.

Early the next day, Lieutenant Grace and Anderssen left Hatfield in the blacksmith's cart, three large canvas-wrapped bundles in the back. They were, said the lieutenant's wife to her particular friend Mrs. Watcham, going to visit a friend of the lieutenant currently stationed on the Press tender in the Thames. There were some things he had found lying around the house he thought Lieutenant Miller might be able to make use of.

Chapter Fourteen

L ife settled down after this incident into something more closely approaching a routine. Georgiana's masters came to the house regularly, and after a few weeks, both the Mrs. Darcys joined in the lessons, the elder having never learned French and the younger wishing to learn to draw so that she might send her husband the sort of delightful sketches he had sent her. It turned out not to be nearly as easy as she had hoped.

Mary came to stay for a month, and at Georgiana's request, her music master listened to her play. Elizabeth would probably have prevented this had she known in advance, for Mr. Haskins was an irascible gentleman. However, while he shook his head and tutted, he also suggested some simple improvements in technique and posture, which made a tremendous difference to Mary's playing. Elizabeth was touched to see how grateful Mary was for even a little attention and consideration, and since Georgiana and she soon became friends, she suggested that Mary share with Georgiana rather than herself. That night she could hear the two girls whispering and giggling together and wondered whether either of them had ever done that before. Marooned between Elizabeth and Jane on the one hand and Kitty and Lydia on the other, Mary had often been left out and, as Elizabeth wrote to her husband, *"I am ashamed of how little consideration I have extended to my poor sister. She is not naturally clever or talented, and in trying to be both, she has made a variety of wrong tacks that Jane and I must endeavour to amend. Is that correct? Tacks?"*

When it was time for Mary to go home, Mrs. Bennet and her remaining daughters came to collect her, bearing letters from Mr. Bennet for Elizabeth to read.

From the first letter:

"The seas were beyond anything I saw when I went to Ireland, even the sailors thought it uncommon rough. I truly thought my cot would be my coffin. However, my son-in-law was very attentive and did everything he could for my comfort. I am fairly certain the Physician to the Fleet thought tending to mere civilians an imposition, but Captain Darcy was not to be gainsaid. Pray tell Lizzy that she has an excellent gentleman for a husband, although I dare say she knows it already."

From the second, headed *The Crown and Anchor, Valletta, Malta*:

After a few paragraphs of description of *"an absurdly English inn in the middle of a Mediterranean town"* and of reassurances about his health, *"the cough almost gone and the ability to breathe deeply I had thought lost forever, regained,"* he again talked of the captain:

Seeing him at his work, I realised what a considerable man he is. The crew he has been given is raw and discontented, the old hands resenting the arrival of the new, and the new confused about their business. However, he has so mixed their duties and their mutual obligations that when he instituted a series of competitions in the various motions that make up their daily activities, such as striking and hoisting the many masts and sails, they were obliged to cooperate and teach the unhandy so as not to lose the match. The prizes are trifling—a bottle of wine, extra duff (a sort of solid pudding), release from punishment—but the good-humoured rivalry is beginning to make an appreciable difference in the feeling amongst the crew.

The officers of the ship have told me of the many cruel and tyrannical captains that abound, men who would enforce obedience with the lash, seeing no other way to control so various a group of men, many of them deeply reluctant to serve, and it is true that I have seen the "grating rigged" for punishment more than once. However, in view of the number of thieves and worse that were included in the latest draft, I am convinced that, on each occasion, it was an absolute necessity and have already noticed that the number of such occasions is sensibly diminishing as time passes.

He sails on his mission—which he refuses to discuss—next week, and I shall miss his company, even though I am very comfortably situated here.

Please send Plotinus, the Eudemian Ethics, and "The Rape of the Lock."

While Elizabeth could have done with more of such information, she could not help but note that her father was quite obviously feeling a great deal better, and she settled down to wait for the next letter from her husband with considerable anticipation.

As she waited, she recruited the small boys of the town as her spies. Every stranger who entered the little town was followed by half a dozen children until he would leave again. The knives-to-grind man had never before worked with an apparently admiring crowd about him and was by no means sure he liked it. The journeyman joiner on the tramp was followed from one end of the town to the other and was glad to leave, although his journey was entirely innocent and his character mild. The potboys at the King's Head and the Eagle and Child and the boy who worked for Mrs. Cope at the little alehouse all reported to Puttnam and received their extra few pennies for doing so. The system was inexpensive and efficient, and Elizabeth was secretly rather proud of it.

After a number of increasingly anxious weeks waiting, two letters arrived from Captain Darcy at once. Lieutenant Grace explained that the ship carrying the first was delayed at sea by an action with a French privateer, which it had chased to Madeira before boarding.

She was feeding the hens when Lieutenant Grace stumped over with the letters and a parcel from her husband. Hurriedly wiping her hands on her apron, she rushed indoors to receive him, scarcely remembering to be civil. Luckily, he seemed to understand, for he soon excused himself and left. Georgiana was at the rectory, learning to dance with the vicar's daughters and some other girls from the town, so she had the letters to herself.

They were numbered "2" and "3," so she opened them in order, glad she had remembered to number her own. The first began, *"Dear Madam,"* and her heart sank.

He began by assuring her of her father's continued improvement. *"I have settled him in the Crown and Anchor, a respectable, quiet place where English is spoken but where he can get the dishes of the region if he so desires. I always think it a shame to visit a place and insist on eating 'the roast beef of old England' and, unlike many of my shipmates, he seems to have no rooted objection to garlic, a herb of the region much used in cookery. He has two rooms and one for Jessup, and he has set his books and papers out quite comfortably. Yesterday, I called to see him and found him sitting outside under an awning, drinking chocolate and watching the life of the port. His breathing is still rather shallower than seems to me quite right, but he can climb the stairs to his room without aid and is taking language lessons from a local schoolmaster."*

There was another charming drawing of her father, in loose trousers and a light jacket over an open-necked shirt, sitting at a table, looking about him, a broad-brimmed hat on the table beside him.

This letter, like her own, was in the form of a journal and it was obvious when her letter arrived, for he broke off a description of a festival in the town for some saint's day or other.

"My Dear Elizabeth, your letter arrived his morning on the Endymion *and was more welcome that you can probably believe."* For a moment, she read no further, a strange feeling in her chest, a sort of hollowness that was still oddly happy. She shook herself and read on:

Not since my mother died have I received a letter so full of home. It was as though you were sitting beside me telling me of your day. I could almost see Anderssen and Grace mending the roof as though it was the foretopmast yard in a heavy swell. If Grace, bless him, has a fault, it is that he does tend to make a fuss when there is anything to be done. I know you will not say anything to him, for he was monstrous kind to me when I was a master's mate, growing out of my uniform and constantly hungry. It was not until many months after I left the Lincoln that I realised that he could not possibly have been sent too much food from home, I was too glad to get the pots of jam he gave me.

You ask why I was sent to sea so very young. It was, I suppose, a mistake. My father was the county MP, and another member, Mr. Gallgrave, mentioned he was sending a lad to sea and did my father want to send his youngest along with him? I found out later that Mr. Gallgrave thought I was rather older than I was, as I was somewhat tall for my age. You must not distress yourself, however. While nine is young, it is by no means unheard of—lads of that age are rated "Captain's Servant" and it is something like an apprenticeship. One learns one's trade by watching and gradually doing more and more as time goes on. Then, when one is twelve or thirteen, one is rated midshipman and given some little authority.

I was luckier than most. The "Illustrious" was a well-run, happy ship, I had a regular allowance of £50 a year sent out, so I was not entirely reliant on ship's stores, and my Uncle Matlock, my mother's brother, was very kind and sent regular presents. So all in all, it could have been a lot worse, especially since I found the mathematics of navigation interesting and, if not easy, then at least possible to be learned, unlike one poor fellow who could never get his brains round it and had to be sent home.

Now, that is a tale from __my__ childhood. You can tell me what your father meant by "never out of a tree."

This seemed to Elizabeth to beg more questions than it answered. Why would a father send a child that young to war? And why did no one write once his mother died?

The rest of the letter was about his life at sea as he tried to mould his miscellaneous crew into an efficient fighting force. *"We have begun to make a little progress at last. The more intelligent amongst the new draft have realised that, although this is a hard life, failing to learn their duty can only make it harder, and they have begun to make an effort to learn. There are still half a dozen hard cases who refuse and a couple of inveterate thieves I have had to have flogged and flogged again for the sake of the ordinary, decent sailors who have little enough without having it stolen. I have always loathed a flogging captain—I see no reason to beat a man for not performing a duty no one has taught him—but any weakness on my part only serves to reduce my authority and make life harder for those who can or wish to do their duty.*

"I would not express any of this aboard, and it is an unexpected comfort to be able to write it to you, my dear Elizabeth."

The end of the letter was abrupt. In the middle of a description of the sailors dancing on the forecastle before hammocks were piped, he broke off to write, *"Williams of the* Swiftsure *calls to say he is homeward bound and will deliver this. Please accept my very best wishes for your continued health and happiness and give my love to Georgiana. Yours, Fitzwilliam Darcy."*

Swiftly, she turned to the second letter:

My Dear Elizabeth,

What on earth is this Georgiana writes about you all being attacked? I read your letter, and I was charmed and soothed by your description of life in a English country town, and the next thing I read is that there was an attempt to cut her out and carry her off!

Please write at once and let me know what really happened. Georgiana wrote something about your wearing her coat, then Puttnam and Anderssen beating

some London roughs and turning them over to the Press. I have read the letter half
a hundred times and can make neither head nor tail of it.

My only consolation is that you appear to have emerged unscathed. Please
extend my thanks to all concerned, but please do not ever hide such things from me
again. At least your (very welcome) letters are intelligible, and I would rather by
far know what is happening at home to those I love than have to guess it from my
sister's letters (perhaps you ought to engage a writing master).

Please write and tell me <u>immediately</u> that you are all safe and well. I have
made some more money available. Tell Anderssen to call in a few more shipmates,
decent reliable men like Haslam and Rattray if he can find them, and billet them
in the stables. A couple of guineas a month and all found would not be too much
for my peace of mind and your safety.

It took several more paragraphs like this before the letter calmed down
enough to contain any news, and Elizabeth was convinced that the first
page had been added to another, rather calmer letter. Her father continued
well, and to everyone's amazement, Jessup was now walking out with the
widow of Mr. Chambers, the former gunner of the *Agamemnon*. "*The lady*
runs a laundry in Valletta and is a much larger woman than he is a man.
However, this does not seem to worry either of them, and they have been seen in
the marketplace, carrying her basket between them, exchanging tender glances
over the handle."

The crew continued to settle, with only a few exceptions:

One poor fellow has gone completely mad and has had to be left at the hospital.
An exceptionally brutish man disappeared overnight, and I suspect the crew gave
him a Jonah's lift over the side. Of course, no one will tell me anything, and I have
had to log him as 'lost at sea.'

However, the majority are shaping reasonably well, and when word comes
that we must sail, we shall be as ready as any other ship in the fleet. We had a
short convoy duty last week, with the wind in just the right quarter and the sea like
milk, and it was the sort of day you dream about on land, when the ship moves like
a living thing and needs only a light hand to give you her best. Half a dozen silly
little galleys tried to cut out the weakest of the convoy, but we soon settled their hash,
which pleased the hands and showed the new men why the gun exercises are so very
important.

We also picked up a French merchant ship on the way home. The cargo was mostly wine and horse furniture, bridles and such, for the French army. So what with that and the head money, you and I shall be better off by another thousand pounds or so as soon as the Admiralty court stirs its stumps and condemns the ship. I am supposed to wait until then before paying anything out to the men, but I have advanced them all a little money from my own funds, which has cheered them even more than the fact that they made four months' pay in one afternoon.

I am sending you and Georgiana some lace I picked up on shore. I am no judge of ladies' requirements, but this strikes me as very handsome, and if it does not suit, perhaps you will accept the wish for the deed. Your father gave me another list of books but, I pointed out that, now he has an address on shore, he can write for them himself. I would not say my esteemed father-in-law has shown himself a reluctant correspondent, but I do not feel an incentive would come amiss.

Then on the last page, after a description of a concert at the Port Admiral's Lodgings, came the news she had not wanted to read.

My orders have arrived at last and I leave on the tide. All being well, I should be back to port within the month, two at the utmost. I am not anticipating any trouble, merely a lack of success; however, we are at war, and no one can know what might happen. If you have not read my will, please do so. I know you will do your best for my sister and her mother, but I want you to be sure to do your best for yourself as well. You deserve so much more than I or the world have given you to date, and if the worst should happen, I will go happier in the knowledge that you are safe, well, and happy.

Please do not forget to write and tell me of your adventures. I hope to be in Malta to read all about it in a few short weeks.

I will only add that you and Georgiana have my dear love and my prayers.

God Bless You,
Fitzwilliam Darcy.

Such a letter was not to be soon recovered from, not least because, when she opened the parcel, she found two beautifully worked but quite different shawls, and she wondered how many men would have taken the time and trouble not to buy identical ones. She had scarcely calmed herself when the request about his will sent her to the bureau. There she found, to her further distress, that he had left her everything he had accumulated in a lifetime at sea, reserving only his godfather's bequest for his sister. If he never came home, she need never be beholden to anyone ever again. With a fortune of over £35,000, she would be able to assist her mother and sisters and buy her own house and even a small estate if she wished.

She did weep then. The thought of that dear, kind, unassuming man so far away, in such a dangerous profession, seemed to her quite suddenly the saddest thing she had ever heard, and it was only the sound of someone rapping on the front door that forced her to recover her countenance and prepare to receive visitors.

Hepszibah came in and bobbed a curtsey. "Lady Catherine de Bourgh and Mr. Collins," she squeaked, and a large, imperious-looking woman swept into the room with Mr. Collins bobbing uneasily in her wake.

"This room is too dark," she said without making or waiting for any greeting. "And that material for the chairs is not at all practical."

Considerably startled, Elizabeth rose, curtsied, and offered her guests seats. Her offer of tea was refused by the lady, although the gentleman looked as though he would have dearly loved to accept.

"You can be at no loss, Mrs. Darcy, to understand the reason of my journey hither," said Lady Catherine as soon as she was seated. "Your own heart, your own conscience, must tell you why I come."

"On the contrary, madam, I am completely at a loss," replied Elizabeth firmly. From the corner of her eye, she saw Mr. Collins blench and shake his head at her. So she turned her face so she could not see him.

Lady Catherine was only checked for a moment and then continued. "Very well, since you refuse to understand me, I have come to ensure the return of that ungrateful child Georgiana to her proper home. When I heard from Mr. Darcy that she had been enticed away from Pemberley by promises of a life independent of the guidance necessary for so young a girl, I was horrified enough. When I heard from Mr. Collins that she had been left in the care of a girl only slightly older than herself, I resolved to fetch the child away immediately. Where is she?"

Despite her best endeavours, Elizabeth could see her cousin's look of triumph, and it was this, as much as the lady's incivility that decided her actions. "Georgiana and her mother are currently at the rectory, taking tea with the vicar's daughters," she replied.

"Then you may send someone to fetch her away. Her packing can begin immediately."

"I shall do nothing of the sort. Georgiana has been left in my care, and I have no intention of permitting her to leave."

Lady Catherine was magnificently outraged, her not inconsiderable bosom swelled, and her voice boomed round the little parlour. "Do you know who I am, young lady? I am Lady Catherine de Bourgh, Mr. Darcy's aunt, and I am not accustomed to being addressed in such fashion."

"My mode of address," retorted Elizabeth, "is entirely prompted by your ladyship's behaviour. Georgiana will stay here, where she, her mother, her brother, and *the law* think her best interests lie."

"I am not so easily dissuaded," said Lady Catherine. "My character has always been marked by firmness of purpose, and I will not leave here without that child."

"You will not leave with her," replied Elizabeth. "And I wonder that your ladyship is not better informed about your nephew Mr. Darcy. When my husband last visited Pemberley, he found his brother's household utterly unsuitable for a young girl, with drink the least of the vices he did not hesitate to lay to his brother's charge."

"Lies!"

"And I wonder that you do not know Captain Darcy better than to accuse him of such falsehoods. However, since I understand his family sent him to sea at the age of nine—yes, madam, nine years of age—and have had little or nothing to do with him thereafter, I suppose I should not be surprised. Now, since you have expressed your purpose and I have refused it, is there anything further to be said?"

It seemed to Elizabeth that Lady Catherine was having difficulty understanding her. Was she really so unused to contradiction? Despite her best endeavours, Elizabeth could not help noticing her cousin's face, open-mouthed and white with shock, and she felt an insane urge to giggle.

"I am not to be spoken to in such a manner! I demand that you produce the child."

"Madam, this is my house, and your manners since you have entered it have hardly been such that I feel at all inclined to pursue the acquaintance." She rose. "Georgiana will stay here with me where I can remedy her recent lack of education and the neglect of her welfare. I bid you good afternoon.

I trust I will not be obliged to send for my men to have you forcibly ejected."

"How dare you!" began Lady Catherine, and she continued in that vein for several minutes. However, in the face of Elizabeth's implacable refusal to change her mind, there was very little the lady could do. Eventually, still expostulating, she rose unwillingly to her feet and made her way for the door with a mutely appalled Mr. Collins in her train. She was still remonstrating at the top of her voice as she left, although the appearance of Anderssen and Puttnam, who must have been summoned by Hepszibah, did at last hurry her into her coach.

As Mr. Collins climbed in behind her, Elizabeth called after him. "By the by, Cousin, I am sure you will be delighted to hear that my dear papa's health is much improved. Indeed, I understand he is as well as he ever was, and we can all look forward to a long and happy life for him." Mr. Collins smiled weakly and disappeared inside with a jerk as the carriage set off, followed by a swarm of fascinated children.

Once back in the house, Elizabeth went upstairs to her bedroom to recover her composure. She laughed and then cried, and by the time Georgiana and the elder Mrs. Darcy returned, she was herself again and able to join in the exclamations over the letters—Georgiana had one of her own—and the shawls, which they all agreed were the prettiest things they had ever seen.

She, of course, hurried to reply to her husband, even though she was not sure when he would receive the letter. "*Dearest Fitzwilliam,*" she wrote, "*I am sorry that Georgiana so worried you, for in truth there was no need. With the help of Anderssen, Puttnam, and dear Lieutenant Grace, the miscreants were dealt with and, I flatter myself, with the minimum of fuss and danger.*" Here she told him the full story, including that of her arrangement of juvenile spies. "*As for the extra men, I shall of course ask Anderssen to do as you wish, although I am not at all sure they will be needed.*"

She also told him of Lady Catherine's visit. "*If she had not arrived just minutes after I had finished your last letter, I am not sure I would have had the courage to be quite so forthright, not to say rude, for she is an imposing figure, and I do not know that I would have realised quite how silly she is had I not been roused by your words.*"

It was difficult to speak of his closing words, but it would have to be done. So after several false starts, she continued:

You cannot know how much my heart was touched by your last letter and, in particular, by its adieu. Please believe me when I say that you have shown yourself to be the kindest and dearest of men, and if, God forbid, I shall be forced to mourn you, then it will be as the husband I had always hoped for and the friend I shall always miss.

God bless you and keep you safe

With fondest love,
Elizabeth

Chapter Fifteen

Once the letter was gone, there was little enough for her to do save start another and wait for news. Lieutenant Grace or Mrs. Grace visited regularly with copies of the *Naval Chronicle,* which were eagerly seized upon. Even if they contained no news, there was a certain satisfaction to be gained from reading his name in the list of Post Captains and watching him slowly climb the ladder of seniority.

When Mary came for another visit at Georgiana's request, Elizabeth learned that Mr. Bingley had proposed to Jane and been refused. "Jane discovered that Mama tried to borrow money from him. Mama has complained forever that Uncle Gardiner will not let her have enough to spend. Jane was horrified and said she is so mortified she can never look him in the face again. Mama was even crosser with her than she was with you and has written to Papa to demand that he come home as soon as ever he can."

Anxious questioning revealed that Jane had cried herself to sleep over it, and Elizabeth racked her brain for a solution and found none that could be conveyed by letter. She understood her sister's feelings but could not help thinking that she was carrying them too far, especially as she understood from Mary that the two young people had discovered a genuine affection for one another. However, she wrote to Jane with as much consolation as she could muster.

Spring arrived. The garden under Puttnam's care began to show the fruits of his labours, and they all enjoyed the early vegetables. Georgiana, to her horror, continued to grow; at fifteen she was already as tall as most women and noticeably taller than Elizabeth. The elder Mrs. Darcy had a birthday and wept as it was celebrated for the first time in many years. Kindness and peace of mind had already gone a long way to dealing with her timidity; an unexpected talent for the French language was expanding her horizons, and she was determined to begin Italian.

Elizabeth had been shocked to learn that George Darcy had demanded a large proportion of Mrs. Darcy's jointure for board and lodgings for herself and Georgiana, and the mere fact that she was now allowed to keep it all seemed to settle her remaining doubts.

Elizabeth was writing of this to her husband one day in early March, Georgiana and Mrs. Darcy were conning their books, and the house was full of the smell of new bread. There was a knock at the door, and the ladies raised their heads from their work when they heard a gentleman's voice talking with Hepszibah. Elizabeth pulled the bell rope, which rang in the stable to alert Anderssen.

"Colonel Fitzwilliam," said Hepszibah, and a tall gentleman of perhaps one- or two-and-thirty entered the room, his reddish curls almost brushing the lintel as he did so.

He bowed generally and said, "Am I addressing Mrs. Darcy—Mrs. Fitzwilliam Darcy?"

Elizabeth got to her feet and curtsied. "Please, sir, do sit down." Her heart was pounding. She wondered whether this was another attempt to reclaim Georgiana and wished she had had the presence of mind to send the girl from the room.

"I don't know whether your husband ever mentioned me. I am his cousin Henry Fitzwilliam. I got your direction from the Admiralty—"

Elizabeth went cold. "Has something happened to my husband?"

"No, no," he hastened to reassure her. "Although I do bring bad news." He glanced at Georgiana. "Of a sort. I'm sorry; I'm making a poor hand of this." He took a deep breath and started again. "I regret to have to tell you that your husband's brother, Mr. George Darcy, died in a fire two weeks ago."

Georgiana gasped and went white. "Was anyone else hurt?" she whispered.

"No, no," he replied. "And very little damage was done to the house, considering. Luckily, the fire was seen, and someone told Mr. Parker, the local magistrate. He went round with some of his people and secured the house. Some rascally servants tried to break into the plate cellar, but he collared them before too much was stolen."

Elizabeth pulled herself together. Surprising news was no excuse for a lack of civility, so she offered her guest tea, which was gratefully accepted. "It is a longer ride from Town than I thought, and when I called in at the King's Head to leave my horse and enquire where you were, I was not made at all welcome."

"I am afraid that is my fault," said Elizabeth, and she explained about her spies.

The colonel thought this an excellent joke and complimented her on the diligence of her network. "We could do with someone like you in Spain," he said. "Half the time, the French know what we are about before we do."

Over tea, he explained how he had become involved. "Mr. Parker knew my father was Mr. Darcy's uncle, so he sent word, and my father went over with some of our people to see what was to be done. He knew I was in London and sent me to the Admiralty to get my cousin's direction. It was there that we found out he had married." He bowed to Elizabeth. "My heartiest congratulations, by the way.

"Since there is no will, your husband inherits the lot, and since it seems you have your husband's power of attorney, we can do nothing without his or your say-so." He looked uncomfortable but ploughed on. "I must admit, for some no doubt foolish reason, I did not expect such a young lady, but the fact remains that there are things that must be decided upon and soon. I came to request you to come to Pemberley with me, though I can see now that this would be most unsuitable."

Elizabeth considered for a moment. This was her husband's inheritance, and quite apart from the need to preserve it, she was possessed of a powerful curiosity to see the place from which he had sprung. "Colonel," she said, "if I can find a suitable escort, would you be prepared to accompany us to Pemberley?"

"Who did you have in mind?" he asked warily.

"Lieutenant Grace is an old shipmate of my husband's, and he and his wife are both neighbours here in Hatfield. If I can persuade them to accompany me, for they are neither of them young, would you come with us?"

At this point, Georgiana interposed that she too wished to go home, and it took the combined efforts of Elizabeth and the colonel to persuade her that this would not be a good idea. "Really, Miss Darcy, the house has been dreadfully neglected," he said. "There are hardly any bedrooms fit for use, and anyone who visits now will have to live in a house on its ears. According to my father, all the family rooms smell dreadfully of smoke."

"There will be nothing for you to do and no one to talk to but me, and I am afraid I shall be very busy," added Elizabeth and it was eventually agreed that Georgiana and her mother would visit Longbourn, at least for a while.

It only remained to agree to meet again in a week's time to begin the journey north.

In the end, it was not Lieutenant and Mrs. Grace who went north with Elizabeth. Two days after the visit from Colonel Fitzwilliam, her Uncle Gardiner arrived with a travelling bag and a letter from Mrs. Parker, wife of the Lambton magistrate and faithful correspondent of Mrs. Gardiner since they were girls together in the village.

"Your aunt Madeleine has told me, quite firmly too I might add, that you are sure to wish to visit Pemberley and that it is my duty to accompany you," he said, insisting that this was a quiet time of year for his business and that he could easily spare two, or even three, weeks to visit Derbyshire. He also brought further details of the fire. "I am sure the colonel was only seeking to spare your feelings, and it would probably be as well if Miss Darcy did not learn of it, but it seems that the poor man set fire to his bed whilst overcome with drink and was unable to save himself." No matter his sins towards his family, this was shocking news indeed, and Elizabeth could find it in her heart to pity him.

Georgiana, though she did not know the details, seemed very little grieved. Indeed, Elizabeth was obliged to reassure her that her fear that she was exhibiting an unnatural indifference to the news was unnecessary, and that she was, in fact, demonstrating the natural reaction of someone treated as she had been for the last few years.

Elizabeth decided not to write to her husband until she had seen his boyhood home and could report in detail about what she found there. She made careful arrangements to have any letters forwarded by express as soon as they arrived and wrote to subscribe to the *Naval Chronicle*, also to be posted straight to Pemberley.

Mr. Gardiner spent the intervening period at Longbourn, suffering with his usual kindly grace the complaints of Mrs. Bennet and consulting with Jane about the business of the estate. Mr. Lester had been his efficient self during the winter, and all was set fair for the coming months; indeed, that gentleman indicated that such was Miss Bennet's administration of the estate that he felt himself surplus to requirements, and unless there were any objections, he would look about for another position and engage for the estate a rather less well-qualified man to do what little work remained.

Georgiana and Mrs. Darcy left for Longbourn, accompanied by Anderssen and the newly arrived Haslam, for no one knew the whereabouts of the miscreant clergyman Wickham. Puttnam stayed at the house, for it would have been cruel to drag him away from his garden, and it was thought as well to have a man stay to keep watch. Elizabeth had never seen herself as a target, and she was confident in the escort of her uncle and of the colonel and his man.

They set off on a bright Tuesday morning. The colonel proved himself to be an easy travelling companion with a fund of interesting conversation about his travels in Spain and Portugal. Mr. Gardiner had considerable interests in the Oporto wine trade, and their mutual familiarity with the country soon broke down any reserve there might have been. Elizabeth had been slightly worried that the colonel might not have taken to a man, no matter how gentlemanly his bearing and behaviour, who made his living from trade. Mrs. Gardiner's correspondent in Lambton had informed her that the colonel's father, and consequently her husband's uncle, was Lord Matlock, the Earl of —, and many men in the same position as the Honourable Henry Fitzwilliam would have been much less friendly and conversable than the colonel.

As she wrote to her husband in the latest portion of her letter/journal, *"Your cousin has been all that is helpful and courteous and has made what might well have proved an uncomfortable journey almost pleasant. My father wrote that every travelling party should include a naval officer, to which I can add that an army officer is of equal utility."*

They were having breakfast at an inn on the morning before they were to arrive at Pemberley when the colonel attempted to prepare her for what she would find. "The house and grounds, while not much damaged by the fire, have been neglected for many years. It appears that my late cousin preferred to hoard his rents rather than spend them on those repairs necessary for every great house, nor did he spend anything on modernising it.

"The prospect and situation are undeniably fine, but there is much that needs to be done to the house, and to the estate as a whole. Luckily, there appear to be considerable monies available for the work, but you are likely to be assailed on all sides by the tenantry who have been unable to undertake any improvements or even repairs." He paused and appeared to be choosing his words carefully. "My father is an excellent gentleman in every respect, but he is somewhat old-fashioned. For example, he would not have corresponded with your husband whilst he was at odds with the head of his family. My original mission to Hatfield was to obtain your consent to his taking over of the estate until such time as your husband comes home from sea. I knew from the moment we met that this was unlikely to meet with your approval." Mr. Gardiner laughed and the colonel looked a little embarrassed. "Please do not think that I myself disapprove; having seen the masterly way you ensured Miss Darcy's peace and safety, I am confident that you are well able to see what must be done and make the necessary decisions. I have endeavoured to express this to my father, but not having had his reply, I cannot say how successful I have been. If he appears a little... impatient, I would ask you bear with him, for whatever his manner, his only desire is to be useful to you and your husband."

Elizabeth was a little taken aback. "I hope, sir, that I will always know how to distinguish good intentions from bad," she said. "And I certainly hope you did not represent me to him as some dreadfully managing termagant. I am well aware that I will need a great deal of help and am only too grateful for any that is offered."

The colonel looked relieved. "In which case, I have a great pile of papers for you to look at, and it occurs to me that we might as well make a start on them as we drive. I saw yesterday that the motion of the coach does not upset you, and there is a lot to be done. I am sure," he added with a bow, "that Mr. Gardiner's assistance will be invaluable."

So that day, as they drove through the countryside that was just springing into bud, he opened a great bag, and they began on its contents. There were questions about tenancies unfilled, rivers silted up, legally obligatory bridge and road repairs not undertaken, dozens of tenant requests, and much correspondence from the parish and the county. It was as much as all three of them could do to arrange them and make memorandum of their contents, and it was obvious that Mr. George Darcy had simply let his correspondence accumulate unanswered; many pages were missing their covers, several letters missing one or more pages, and an unpleasant number were stained with food and wine.

This occupied the party for the rest of the day. They stopped only briefly at noon for a hurried meal, and it was getting late in the afternoon when they finally arrived at Pemberley. The gatehouse was empty and the road unkempt, but the woods through which they drove were glorious, and Elizabeth breathed in the scent of the new leaves and promised herself hours of happy rambling. She spun round in her seat as they passed a glade with a carpet of new daffodils and, when she sat back, saw her uncle watching her, his expression affectionate.

Then they turned a corner, and there was the house. It was not, as Elizabeth had half-expected, in the modern Palladian style, all smooth stone and great symmetrical pillars. This was an older building from the period when James Stuart first came down from Scotland, and it was wholly beautiful, from the barley-sugar twist chimneys, past the many-paned windows, to the overgrown knot garden in front, the whole built in a golden stone that caught the setting sun.

The colonel rapped on the carriage roof and ordered a halt so that she could drink it in. "I was afraid you might find it old-fashioned," he said softly.

"No," she breathed. "I find it…" She struggled for words before choosing, "magnificent." She saw him heave a sigh of relief.

"So many people are prey to the mania for improvement," he said, "I last saw it as a boy at your father-in-law's funeral, and I thought then it was a jewel." He rapped on the roof again, and they drove down to the stable courtyard.

Closer to the house, the years of neglect were more visible. Grass grew between the cobbles in the yard, and there were slates, or rather great sheets of stone, missing from the stable roofs. The house too showed signs of un-repaired damage, windows had been boarded over, and some were entirely blocked by ivy.

As she endeavoured to explain in her letter, "*Your cousin thinks I am dazzled, and I am, but not so dazzled that I do not see that there is much work to be done. We will start tomorrow to assess the damage. However, none of it detracts from the beauty. The house is like a handsome woman who has let her face grow dirty and her clothes ragged; it is all on the surface, and underneath there is such loveliness.*

"*I know no decision has been made as to what to do with the house, and while I cannot conceive of anyone willingly selling such a place, I know that decision rests with you. However, even if you are minded to sell, the property will fetch a much higher sum if it is in good order, and I have resolved to do my utmost to bring it to such a condition."*

That night they slept in three of the guest bedrooms, well away from the room where the fire had taken place. Servants were there from the Matlock family home at Alfreston, and they had done their best in the time available, though they were few and there was much that needed doing.

Lord Matlock drove over in time for breakfast the next morning, and Elizabeth could see how easily his manner might have been misunderstood. *"Your uncle was indeed a little brusque when he arrived,"* she wrote, *"and if it had not been for the colonel's warning, I might well have taken it amiss. However, once I expressed my gratitude for his help and requested his further counsel, he hemmed and hawed once or twice, and we soon became the best of friends. He is astonishingly like you, you know. He has your height and, although it is more grey than black, your hair. I wonder where the colonel's red curls come from."*

The first order of business was the house. Apart from anything else, Georgiana was anxious to return to her childhood home, especially now that the source of all its unpleasant memories was gone. Remembering the few times her sister had spoken of Pemberley, Elizabeth enquired whether the former housekeeper, Mrs. Reynolds, was still to be found in the area. Mr. Gardiner tracked her to her brother's farm on the other side of Lambton, and Elizabeth persuaded her to return and help set the house to rights.

In Mrs. Reynolds' wake came a growing stream of former servants, discharged by the late owner but willing to return. Mr. Gardiner reduced the household's books to something like order, and Elizabeth was able to access the funds that had been hoarded and set them to work. Craftsmen came from nearby towns and started upon the repairs, the ivy was carefully torn away, and the house began to shine once more. The master's apartments were stripped to the rafters and joists and the whole remade so that most of the former bedroom became the dressing room and other offices.

As predicted, the tenants soon began to arrive, and Elizabeth had to beg for their patience. At Mr. Gardiner's suggestion, she sent for Mr. Lester, who rode the estate for her and made up a schedule of the most urgent works for her to inspect. The colonel drove out with her, Mr. Gardiner making one of the party for propriety's sake, although as he pointed out himself, the countryside was by no means his *metier*. There was some grumbling, especially from those tenants whose concerns were not to be immediately addressed; however, a meeting of the tenantry was called at which Lord Matlock presided, and the grumbling largely quieted.

Georgiana and Mrs. Darcy arrived home just in time for Mr. Gardiner to leave, having neglected his own business for too long. *"I shall miss my Uncle Gardiner,"* she wrote, *"not only for his business acumen and steady good humour but for his confidence in me. He seemed to conceive of no reason why I should not manage, so I have told myself there is no reason why I should doubt myself. The colonel is ordered to return to London, and we shall all miss him. Luckily, Lord Matlock, or Uncle Alfred as he told Georgiana and me to call him, will visit regularly, and he assures me that I can request his assistance at any time."*

Colonel Fitzwilliam undertook to take this latest letter to London and have it sent through Admiralty channels, so she ended it:

We have not heard from you for several months, and though there is no bad news in the Chronicle, I cannot help but grow anxious. I know you will not keep us unnecessarily in suspense, but I look to hear from you that you are safe and well and on the way home to those who love you.

Amongst whom are numbered your devoted wife,
Elizabeth

PS. Your cousin is to take this to London. I hope it will not be delayed because I did not send it by Lieutenant Grace.

Weeks passed, and still there was no word. The house and gardens were approaching their original magnificence and even Mrs. Reynolds was almost satisfied. "If you could only have seen it when Lady Anne had the running of it," she said one day as she and Elizabeth were going over the household accounts. "It is almost there now, but still…"

"Did you know my husband when he was a boy?" asked Elizabeth, setting down her pen.

"Oh yes, madam. I was stillroom maid then, but I used to see him about the place. Handsome lad he was, even then and so sweet natured. I don't think I ever heard him say a cross word."

"Then perhaps you can tell me why he went to sea so very young. I confess I have always wondered."

Mrs. Reynolds pursed her lips. "I don't hold with gossip, ma'am, as well you know," she said. "And they do say you should never speak ill of the dead." It was obvious to Elizabeth that she was only waiting to be persuaded, so she did her best.

"Well," said Mrs. Reynolds after several minutes of appeal to her knowledge of the family, "Mr. Darcy—old Mr. Darcy that is—was never what you'd call an affectionate man. I don't mean he was cruel or vicious, not like Mr. George—God rest his soul—just not tender or considerate to his family or anyone else for that matter. He was one of those men—Mr. Tanner of High Farm is another—who don't need any pleasure or comfort or affection in their lives. And don't see why anyone else needs them either." She settled back in her chair and got confidential.

"Someone offered Master Fitzwilliam a place on a ship, so off he had to go, for all Lady Anne was heartbroken. He was terribly severe with Mr. George too—had to be always moiling at his books, no hunting, no going to assemblies, no going to London. It's hardly a surprise he cut loose as soon as he could."

"And my husband's mother? I've seen her portrait upstairs; what was she like?"

Mrs. Reynolds considered. "She was beautiful, but…well, she was sad. The marriage was not of her choosing, and he was not the husband for her. She should have had someone gentle and good-humoured, and he was neither. She loved her boys though. I used to see her sitting at that very desk, writing to Master Fitzwilliam and drawing him little pictures." Then, obviously thinking she had said too much, she added, "Now, about the music room, do you want me to send for the piano tuner?"

Haymaking came and went, and still there was no news. Colonel Fitzwilliam and Lord Matlock visited and expressed their surprise at how much had been done. She continued to write her letters and send them off, but no reply came, and she scoured the newspapers for word from the Mediterranean.

She did receive one strange letter, however, from the office of the Bishop of Derby. It requested Captain Darcy to appoint someone else to the living at Kympton in view of the "*absence of the previous appointee who, I understand, has not been seen for several months, having left on a visit to London and not returned. All enquiries in the capital have produced no news as to his whereabouts, and the bishop feels that it is inadvisable to leave the parish without spiritual direction."*

Elizabeth's own inquiries at Kympton revealed that no one had seen the Reverend Mr. Wickham for some time, and the pot-boy at the King George in Lambton told Anderssen that no one had seen him since "'e climbed into the London coach in one of they driving coats with the extra shoulder cloaks." Although that sounded an awful lot like the "driving coat" who had taken part in the attack in Hatfield, Elizabeth decided that there was no way to be certain and, in the meantime, they would continue to take precautions. This meant that, although she greatly disliked it, either Anderssen or Haslam followed at a distance every time she walked in the woods.

She was returned from one such walk when she saw an express rider galloping towards the house. She picked up her skirts and ran as fast as she could, arriving in the great hall to see Mrs. Reynolds paying off the rider. It was indeed a letter in her husband's dear, familiar writing. She hurried into the library and sank down on the window seat to read it. She tore open the cover and thought her heart would stop. It began *"Dear Madam."*

Chapter Sixteen

T he letter was headed *"Aboard* HMS Achilles, *Gibraltar"*:

> *May I first express my profound gratitude for your manifold kindnesses to my sister and her mother? And for the highly effective measures you have taken to ensure their safety and comfort. I am also mindful of the debt I owe you with regard to Pemberley. It would indeed grieve me to know that my boyhood home had been allowed to decay and that the people connected with it were suffering from the deficiencies of my family.*

Her breath seemed to have become thick and difficult to draw. How could he talk of gratitude after so many months of silence between them? She read on.

> *My recent mission was attended with that lack of success that I so often prophesied, and the "Achilles" is currently undergoing further repair at Gibraltar. I regret I was unable to call in at Malta to visit Mr. Bennet; however, a shipmate who was recently in Valletta assures me of his continuing good health, having seen him making one of a party to visit some ruins in the interior of the island. I rejoice that I have been able to repay some of your kindness in this manner.*
>
> *As for myself, I am returning to England only briefly before taking command of the frigate "HMS Vanguard," one of the new heavy frigates built on the American model. It is unlikely that I will return to England for some time.*
>
> *In that connection it occurs to me that, with the recent death of my unfortunate brother, the matter of my sister's custody is no longer at issue and, since our marriage was never consummated...*

She could read no further through her tears and was obliged to leave off and search for a handkerchief. Finding none, she wiped her eyes on her sleeve and continued.

... since our marriage was never consummated, it is possible, and indeed incumbent upon me, to release you from an arrangement whose utility is now dubious. Your recent letters have demonstrated that a lady of your ability will never lack for admirers, and I am sure you will soon be able to embark upon a marriage in every way more suitable. There is, of course, no question of repaying the settlement made upon you, which will, I hope, enable you to embark upon a new sphere of life.

On receipt of your agreement, I will write to my Uncle Matlock and request him to take Georgiana and her mother into his household. I regret that the estrangement between my brother and my Fitzwilliam relations prevented such an arrangement before you and I were obliged to take such drastic measures to preserve her. Your Mr. Lester seems a gentleman admirably placed to undertake the administration of the estate, reporting to Lord Matlock where appropriate. I understand from your letter that my uncle was prepared to act in this manner before your arrival rendered his assistance unnecessary. However, it would be most ungenerous of me to expect you to continue as you have when you must be desirous of your own establishment.

Mere words cannot express my consciousness of your forbearance to date, and it is for this reason that I will not and cannot demand anything further of you. I understand that it will be necessary to make a declaration before the appropriate ecclesiastical authorities, and I await only your written consent to make the necessary preliminary enquiries.

I remain, madam, your humble and obedient servant,
Fitzwilliam Darcy

For the first time in her life, she thought she might faint. There was a tingling sensation in her face and hands, and darkness seemed to be gathering at the edges of her mind. This could not be true. She bent forward and pressed the heels of her hands to her eyes. She could not think. She could barely breathe for the weight pressing on her chest.

There was a noise. Someone was knocking. She had to clear her throat before she could bid the person enter. It was Mrs. Reynolds, looking concerned.

"Are you all right, ma'am?" she asked nervously. "Anderssen says he heard you call out, and I've been knocking for some while."

Elizabeth's thoughts seemed to have slowed, and it felt like several minutes passed before she could answer. "I am not feeling very well," she said. "I believe I will go and lie down for a while. There is no need to alarm Miss Darcy." She was conscious that her voice sounded strained, but there was nothing she could do about that. She got to her feet, and some part of her was surprised they would bear her. Walking like a woman three times her age, she slowly made her way upstairs and lay down on the bed in her new room, blind to its comfort and beauty. Her thoughts had settled down to a dull roaring noise like the sea, which gradually drowned out all conscious attempts to make sense of what she had read. She slept.

It was almost dark when she awoke, and she was dimly conscious that a door had just closed—Georgiana, no doubt, checking that she was well. There was a heavy weight on her thoughts, and it was several minutes before she could bring herself to rise and wash her face. Maria came in when she rang and was touchingly glad to see her up and about, and Elizabeth had no doubt that the news would soon be spread downstairs.

According to Aunt Phillips's clock, which cut a decidedly plebeian figure in her new rooms, it was almost time for supper, and she hoped Georgiana or perhaps Mrs. Reynolds had seen to its ordering. For herself, the mere thought of food was nauseating, but she knew she must make the attempt for the sake of those who depended upon her. The memory that they might not so depend for much longer struck like a knife, making her gasp.

Warm water and a fresh gown went some way to reviving her, and she managed to take her place at table, assuring her little family that it was only a passing indisposition. She could not bring herself, as yet, to inform them of the letter—tomorrow, perhaps, when she had forced herself to understand it. She managed to eat enough to satisfy the most affectionate scrutiny and then, pleading a continuing headache, retired for the night. She knew she would not sleep. It was time to think. She had often been called intelligent, perceptive, and even clever; now was the time to apply all the gifts of intellect the Almighty had bestowed.

The letter was still on the floor of her bedroom where it had dropped from her despairing grasp while she slept. Carefully, she smoothed out the creases and carried it over to her dressing table where candles burned in extravagant profusion. The handwriting caused a dreadful pang, but she thrust that aside to consider the matter contained in the letter.

As she read, she felt the first stirrings of something that felt very much like anger. There was so much about it that was puzzling, especially when set against the conversational and affectionate warmth of his previous letters. After several readings, she dismissed the first two paragraphs as mere civilities, the bare minimum possible in a gentleman's correspondence, although she made a note to pass on to Longbourn the comment about her father.

The appointment to *HMS Vanguard* in the next paragraph had not appeared in the *Naval Chronicle* which she had received only the previous day; however, it would appear there in due course so that, quite apart from the difficulty she had in seeing him as a bald-faced liar, the statement was subject to corroboration and therefore had to be accepted as true.

The meat of the difficulty lay in the next two paragraphs. What on earth did he mean by *"Your recent letters have demonstrated that a lady of your ability will never lack for admirers"*? The only gentlemen she had mentioned had been her Uncle Gardiner, Lord Matlock, and Mr. Lester, who were married, and the colonel. Surely to heaven, he was not suggesting some sort of attachment had grown between them? She had laid her heart on every page of her last few letters, letters she knew he had received since he mentioned the restoration of Pemberley. What sort of woman did he think she was?

She got up so she could pace about the room, for she could feel the anger now, hot and unmistakeable. And the rest of it, the subtle suggestion that she had taken too much upon herself, the mention of money that came perilously close to payment for services rendered. How dare he! What sort of man was he? It was impossible that the gentle loving man who had written the previous letters should have written this...this...dismissal.

And then she had it, and the relief cut her legs from under her so that she sat down on the floor in a heap. Yes, it *was* impossible. It was unmistakeably his hand, his way of writing a single "s" where two were needed and then squeezing the extra one in, his hand, his words and yet not *him*, not the true, the inner Fitzwilliam Darcy. Something else was at work here—something she did not as yet understand but most certainly would before very long. It was long past eleven o'clock, but she took a candlestick, went down to the library, and searched out the last *Naval Chronicle*. There had been much discussion of the new design of the *Vanguard* and yes, there it was: a note that the ship was currently in the hands of the riggers and caulkers and was expected to be provisioned and ready for sea at Portsmouth by the end of the month.

She took her candle and returned to her bed, apologising in passing to a bleary-eyed Haslam who had come to see who was moving about the house. Tomorrow she would send him—no, tomorrow she would send one of the grooms on horseback to all her neighbours to beg copies of every newspaper they had, and she would write to Uncle Gardiner. He had correspondents in the merchant service; perhaps he could help, for she was certain it was something that had happened at sea. She knew herself to be far from perfect but could think of nothing she had done that could possibly have called forth such a dreadful letter.

Something had happened between her husband leaving Malta on his mission and his writing from Gibraltar. She had three weeks to find out what it was, and then she would act.

Chapter Seventeen

The next day, Pemberley was a hive of activity. Grooms rode out to beg, borrow, or steal newspapers, the family chaise was disinterred from the stable where it had rested for the last ten years, and an express was sent to Mr. Gardiner in Gracechurch Street. To Georgiana and her mother, she said only that her husband would be in England for but a brief time, and that she would dearly love to spend that time alone with him. Georgiana, although disappointed, was neither so ungrateful nor so insensible that she did not understand the request, and she settled down to writing a monstrous great letter and to drawing as much of the restored Pemberley as she could manage in the time allowed.

Elizabeth poured over the newspapers and the back issues of the *Naval Chronicle* and gathered little. The *Vanguard* was described at length and the name of her future captain speculated upon for, in the words of one of the *Chronicle*'s correspondents, *"a more 'plum' posting it would be hard to conceive, and the man who finds himself posted to this magnificent ship will surely be distinguished either for his parts or for potent interests on shore, pressing for his promotion."*

Although her mind was much oppressed with speculation and anxiety, Elizabeth did not neglect the business of the house and estate. A conference with Mr. Lester and another with Mrs. Reynolds ensured that all would proceed smoothly, with particular care being taken to celebrate Georgiana's sixteenth birthday. She wrote to Lord Matlock, reminding him of this happy event in the hopes that he would ride over and perhaps invite the two ladies to visit his home, Alfreston Park. Anderssen and Haslam were to stay at Pemberley to guard Georgiana if necessary, and Elizabeth would travel through Hatfield and take up Puttnam to act as guide. It would be cruel indeed to expose the able-bodied seamen to the dangers of the Press.

Although it felt like hubris of the worst sort, she did not neglect herself. She had already ordered from the dressmaker in Lambton the most becoming of travelling clothes and gowns for wearing in the day. Half in shame and half in bravado, she had also ordered a nightgown of such translucent daring that she was by no means sure she would ever venture to wear it. The promise of an additional generous fee ensured that the remainder of the items would be supplied as soon as possible. She had originally ordered the clothes for his longed-for return home, to look as beautiful as she might. Now, as Maria alternately packed and pleaded to be allowed to accompany the party, Elizabeth tried not to imagine a journey home, when all this finery was revealed for the desperate throw she suspected it might prove to be.

Mr. Gardiner's reply when it came was not such as to aid in calming her spirits. It arrived the day before she had determined she must leave for Portsmouth and enclosed a copy of the latest edition of *The Times*.

He wrote, "*I have been unable to discover much more than is written in these pages. There are rumours of great changes at the department of the Admiralty in charge of intelligence, consequent upon some as yet announced failure on its part. Please write as soon as you can. In the meantime, your aunt and I and the children will keep you both in our prayers.*"

She tore the newspaper open, her eyes darting about its pages. She was so flurried that it took her several minutes to find the report headed "*Naval Engagement in the Mediterranean.*"

"*We are informed,*" it began, "*that an engagement took place at sea off the island of— between His Majesty's Ship* Achilles *and the French national ship of war* La Gloire, *accompanied by a number of lesser vessels from states allied to the French.*" To Elizabeth's shocked gaze, the list of additional ships seemed horribly long. "*The* Achilles *was present to meet with parties thought eager to shake off the yoke of Corsican tyranny; however, we regret to say that, due to a culpable laxity in the arrangements, from which we do not hesitate to acquit the ship and its gallant officers and men, the appointment was widely known and much canvassed in Malta and doubtless other parts where British naval business is conducted.*

"*We understand that Captain Darcy of the* Achilles *brought this to the attention of the naval authorities in those parts, but there was present no superior officer with the courage to overrule orders from London, and the ship was forced to sail for a meeting which many aboard must have suspected would prove not only fruitless but dangerous.*

"*The result is easy to foresee. The appointment was a trap, and it is only the bravery and seamanship of those aboard which brought the ship away, although the expense in men and materiel is impossible to exaggerate. There are reported killed 52, including Mr. T Pascoe - First Lieutenant, Mr. M Hannaside - Sailing Master ...*" The column of names reached the bottom of the page and included names familiar to Elizabeth from her husband's letters. She could only guess at the anguish such losses would cause to the men who had been their shipmates. "*... many dying in the days after the battle from their wounds. Also wounded, 36. This from a ship's complement of only 284.*

"*No greater tribute to the fallen can be given than to report that* La Gloire *was forced to flee and that two smaller vessels* [their names and details were given at length] *were taken prizes. We understand that the* Achilles *will require substantial repair and Captain F Darcy will transfer to the new ship* HMS Vanguard.

"*Although no man who serves his country in time of war expects that service to be always safe or easy, it is to be hoped that the gallant men of the* Achilles *will not again face more danger at the hands of their friends than they do at those of their enemies.*"

This was worse, much worse than Elizabeth had feared, and she was at once wild to be off. Hiding the report from Georgiana was imperative, and any longer delay would only increase the chance that she would miss her husband altogether.

Within the hour, the coach was ordered round, trunks and bags packed aboard, and a rider dispatched to order horses prepared at their first stopping place. Mr. Lester produced a considerable sum of money for the journey, and all was prepared. Her last sight of Pemberley was of Georgiana standing forlornly on the front steps, waving her handkerchief and attempting, with indifferent success, not to cry.

For once in her life, money was no object to Elizabeth, and they swept south as fast as the horses could gallop. Frequent changes, a moonlit night, and good roads saw them dash into Hatfield not thirty hours later. Putnam was collected, assuring her as he climbed unwillingly inside that no further letters of any description had been received. She did not wait to call at Longbourn, dearly though she would have loved to see Jane, but set off south again, determined to reach the first tollgate on the road west as soon as might be.

As they raced through the countryside, Puttnam forever asleep opposite her, she attempted to subdue the wild imaginings of her heart. They travelled at such speed that reading was impossible and sleep only available to the exhausted or insensible. Time and again, she stepped from the coach to stretch stiffened limbs while the horses were changed or attempted to snatch a bite to eat, and time and again, she begrudged every second she was not upon the road.

The ten hours between London and Portsmouth seemed to her the longest day she had ever spent. At the post boy's recommendation, the Darcy chaise pulled into an inn known for accommodating naval officers ashore, and Puttnam stumped in to make enquiries. He came back within minutes.

"He's 'ere, ma'am," he said, and Elizabeth felt again the terrible hollowness of anticipation. "Leastwise, 'e's expected back from the dockyard later tonight." She climbed from the chaise; her legs felt weak beneath her, and she was pathetically glad for a brief respite before she saw him.

She took rooms at the rear of the house, and the chambermaid helped her out of clothes and into bed. She had persuaded the inn servants not to mention her arrival to her husband, for instinct told her he might well flee her presence, out to some ship where she could not follow. So she told them her arrival was to be a surprise, and since they knew he was no libertine who might be surprised with a woman of the town, they took her coins and promised their silence with indulgent smiles. It was agreed that Puttnam would send the chambermaid to wake her the minute he arrived.

To her surprise, she slept deeply, and it was dark before the tap came on her chamber door. She dressed hurriedly but well, not ashamed to use every weapon in her arsenal. If he intended to set her aside, he would be brought to recognise what he had chosen to discard. She was so hurried that there was scarcely time to be afraid before she stepped out into the corridor to meet Puttnam. He took her to the next floor, and she was just in time to see a door open and a man who looked like a clerk come out.

"And tell those crooked hounds at the Victualling Board I know all their tricks. I am not to be bribed, and I am not to be practised upon." It was his voice, strong and alive, and her knees weakened. The door shut, and she summoned the courage to approach it. However, before she could do so, Starkey came up the backstairs with a tray of food in his hands, the captain's belated supper. He did not see her until she came round her corner, just as he knocked on the door and announced his errand.

She thought she heard him whisper some words of thankfulness for her arrival but she could not hear them. All she heard was *his* voice from within, bidding her enter. She took the tray from Starkey's hands, and he opened the door for her.

The captain was sitting at a table covered with official-looking books and papers. He was in his shirtsleeves and had loosened his stock; his eyes were closed, and he was resting his head against the back of the chair in utter weariness. Everything was made plain to her. His face—his dear, kindly, strong face—was ruined. A great scar covered the left side, from forehead to lips, obliterating one eye and twisting the corner of his mouth into an ugly sneer. He had grown his hair long to conceal it, but the puckered, pockmarked skin and his horribly damaged ear were still visible.

"Fitzwilliam," she said softly, and instantly he swept the candle to the floor and plunged the room into darkness.

There was silence, and she could hear her heart beating. She bent and set the tray on the floor and listened.

"You should not have come, ma'am," he said at length.

"Did you really think I would care?" she said, prepared for battle.

"You should care," he answered harshly. "I care. Every man and woman I meet cares. They cannot look at me, and then they cannot look away. I repulse people, even here in Portsmouth where such sights are common."

This was easy. "They may care if they wish, but they do not love you. I love you, Fitzwilliam." She heard his indrawn breath. "I love *you*, the gentle man, the generous man, the brave, loving—"

"I want no pity," he interrupted fiercely.

"And for fear of pity you will turn away love?" The words were easy, flowing from somewhere deep inside her. "Oh, you *foolish* man. I am not a child to worry over appearances. I love you; I think I have loved you for a very long time." Her eyes were becoming accustomed to the darkness now, and she saw him rise to his feet, silhouetted against the stars filling the window behind him.

"How can I ask any woman to kiss this mouth?"

"I shall kiss that mouth a thousand, thousand times," she said, and in two strides, she was in his arms.

She could feel the linen of his shirt beneath her cheek and, under that, the pounding of his heart. His face was buried in her hair, and he was murmuring her name over and over again. "Lizzy, Lizzy, Lizzy." She put her arms about his waist, feeling the hard muscles of his back flex. There were scars here too. He was, she realised, trembling, so she lifted her head for his kiss. Yes, his lips did feel strange, but it was his breath, his tongue in her mouth, and compared to that, what else mattered?

It was he who broke off first, his breathing ragged. "I did not think... no one has ever..." he began, and she knew he had never been the first consideration for anybody, had never known what it was to be the centre of anyone's thoughts.

"You are mine!" she said fiercely. "And I will always be yours, and I am not to be set aside."

She heard his breath hitch in a soft chuckle. "No, ma'am."

"And we are not going to get an annulment!"

"Lizzy, have you really thought..."

"I have spent the last two weeks imagining horrors, nothing you can say or do—" This time *he* silenced *her* with a kiss that set her head whirling. "And you do not want me to go, do you?" she added breathlessly.

"God help me, I know I ought, but no, I do not want you to go, ever." He was rocking her in his arms, his voice muffled in her hair. The trembling slowly abated until, in the silence, they both heard her stomach rumble and burst out laughing.

They fumbled around on the floor, found the candle, and called for a light and more supper. They ate at the table, the papers swept aside for the moment, and if he preferred her to sit on his uninjured side, she was not going to be so cruel as to comment upon the fact, especially if it meant that they could hold hands between mouthfuls.

"Will you tell me what happened?" she asked as they pushed their plates away.

He shrugged. "It was a slaughter," he said simply. "I knew it would be, but the prize had we succeeded would have helped end this war so much earlier, so I felt I had to make the attempt. They were waiting for us in force, and we had to fight our way free." He took a deep draught of his wine. "We did as much as any man can hope to do, and we died in our dozens. I have seen war at sea before; I have seen nothing like this."

"And your injuries?" she asked, her heart aching.

He waved a hand, as though dismissing his wounds. "One of the stern chasers exploded. I was half turned away so it was not as bad as it might have been." He looked down into his glass. "Hannaside killed himself at Gibraltar; he lost his sight and could not bear it. I have little enough to complain about."

She placed a hand over his clenched fist. "And must you go back to sea?"

"We are at war, my love. I do not see how I can honourably stay ashore." He placed a hand over hers. "Not an hour ago, I was longing to be gone. Now..." He got to his feet to stride about the room. "This war cannot last much longer. Wellington is at the gates of France, and the Russians and their allies approach from the east. I accepted command of the *Vanguard* on the assurance that, once the war was over, we would be sent to Africa to help suppress the slave trade." He turned to look at her. "It is noble work and work I could do well, but now? How can I leave you when I have just found you?" She opened her mouth to reply, but before she could do so, he spoke again.

"Come with me!" he said. "We shall be based at Freetown in Sierra Leone. I would be at sea most of the time, but we could take a house there, and I would come home as often as I could."

She stared at him, eyes wide. "I couldn't," she said. "Could I?"

"Why not?" His enthusiasm was rising. "There is a garrison and an English governor and settlement. And after a few years, when the navy has settled down into a peacetime establishment, and good, trustworthy, zealous men are in want of employment, we can go home to Pemberley."

"But...but...what about Georgiana and her mother?"

He leaned over and rifled through the papers on the table. "I have a letter here from my uncle, offering to give all three of you a London Season. I am sure he would be happy to care for them both; he writes how much my aunt is looking forward to having some ladies about the house. Come with me, Lizzy—come to sea."

She met him in the middle of the room, fired by his rising excitement. "And would you have me live on salt horse and Old Weevil's Wedding Cake?"

He laughed at that. "Anderssen?"

"Lieutenant Grace."

"We can do a little better than that, my love." He took her hands in his and kissed them both. "Come and see my world, Lizzy. Life at sea, the good and the bad. Come and see the world, see Africa, flowers and trees with leaves like flames, moths the size of your hand, birds every colour of the rainbow, and at night you can hear the leopards—they don't roar, you know, they cough." She was laughing now; he stood in the middle of the room, waving his arms about like a boy. "And the people. They come from all over Africa. People talk a great deal of nonsense about savages—there are dozens of different tribes and races, as many as there are Europeans, all with their different lives. And the music at night—great hollow musical drums and pipes and little harps. Come listen with me." He kissed her as she laughed, and he was laughing with her.

Recklessness seized her; a broader, more vivid life exploded before her startled mind's eye. "Yes," she said beneath his kisses. "Yes, I'll come with you."

He heaved her off her feet and spun her round in the air with a triumphant "Yes!" and then they were kissing again. There was joy and a burning in her heart, and suddenly there was no more room for laughter. He held her head between his hands. "Will you stay with me tonight?" he whispered and felt her try to nod.

His bed was next door, his nightshirt laid out, only to be swept onto the floor. She had to tell him how to loosen her clothes, both of them giggling breathlessly as he complained that surely so many layers were not necessary, and if this were a fair-weather rig, he would hate to unwrap her from her storm canvas.

Skin on skin stopped the laughter again. There was no candle burning, but the curtains were drawn apart, and she could see his awed face in the moonlight as he touched and discovered her with gentle, eager hands. He tried to say something of his gratitude, his love, but she stopped his mouth with hers and then neither of them spoke for a very long time. She had completely forgotten her mother and Mrs. Gardiner, and expecting no pain, she felt none, only a gathering excitement, a building heat and a sudden, strange, wondrous, unexpected rush of something she decided was love, which shook them both and left them breathless and whispering on the same pillow.

"So much for the annulment," she said with satisfaction and heard him groan and laugh into the pillow. "And I have wasted twelve guineas on a most unladylike nightgown which I see I shall never need."

Her hand was on his face, and she felt him raise his untouched eyebrow. "I think I should still be allowed to see it worn, if only to see how unladylike a nightgown it could be." He looked at her more closely. "Are you blushing, my dear? Now, I really want to see it." He overcame her attempt to hit him with the pillow by the simple expedient of taking her in his arms and kissing her thoroughly.

It was, he was forced to agree the following night, a most unladylike article indeed and, in his opinion, twelve guineas very well spent.

The Epilogue

The news had reached her long before the ship dropped anchor, so that when he arrived, he found her sitting on the veranda in a simple white dress. A stout infant of three summers was playing nearby with her particular friend, the cook's son, who, despite having two perfectly good names of his own (one African, one European), was universally known as Heckle, having been so christened by the commodore's daughter, the undisputed monarch of the house.

He was in his shirtsleeves, his uniform coat slung over his shoulder to be instantly discarded as soon as his womenfolk saw him.

"Pampam!"

"Fitzwilliam."

He swung his daughter round his head, smiling as she screamed in delight, and then balanced her on one hip so he could kiss his wife. He was burnt a deep brown by the sun and, in the gloom, one hardly noticed the scars or the still-closed eye. There was certainly no lack of ardour in his kiss. The suggestion of dinner was scornfully rejected, and the commodore carried his wife up to their room for an immediate reunion, leaving little Jane and Heckle to run and greet Starkey, who could usually be relied upon to have something interesting or tasty about him.

It was several hours and a very belated supper later before they had occasion for much conversation, beyond those protestations somewhat unusual between man and wife married for very nearly five years. They were still lying in their great bed, surrounded by netting against the many insects that came out at night, watching an enormous tropical moon rise over the trees.

"Is there any news from home?" he asked lazily.

"Heavens, yes, the packet came in two weeks ago. Let me see. Georgie writes from Alfreston to say that she does not want to marry Sir Richard after all..."

"I knew it!"

"And that Uncle Alfred is plotting to undermine the government..."

He raised his head to look at her, mildly interested. "Again?" he asked.

"Again." He dropped down to lie on his back, stretching luxuriously in a bed so much larger than any he could count on at sea. "Oh, and her mother is being courted by someone she says is called Mr. Scrape, although that hardly seems likely."

"There used to be a family in the neighbourhood called Scrope; perhaps it's one of them."

"Scrope, much more likely. What else? Um...Jane and Charles are thinking of giving up Netherfield, as Mama will insist on visiting. Mama still thinks we ought to go home before we are eaten by cannibals and Papa is threatening to let Longbourn and go back to Malta. He says she and Kitty can go and live with Mary and Mr. Hilliard in Hatfield—although I cannot imagine Mr. Hilliard agreeing to that. Oh, and Lydia says can you lend her husband a thousand pounds—I wrote back no, by the way."

A long, heavy arm pulled her into his side. "Quite right too. What on earth does he want a thousand pounds for?"

"I imagine it's one of his silly schemes, probably a perpetual motion machine or a device for extracting sunbeams from cucumbers or something equally foolish. I always wondered what sort of man would marry Lydia, and now I know." She rested her head on his chest and watched her finger wandering down his stomach to his navel. "I hope you remembered to bring your linen ashore to be washed this time."

He pulled her finger up and kissed the end. "This time I am bringing more than my linen ashore," he said and grunted as she sat up with the aid of an elbow in his chest. "The *Holdfast* met the squadron two days out with new orders. Colbourne is here to take over as commodore, and we can go home. So, my love, shall we take the next packet or would you rather wait for a month or two and take passage on a nice commodious Indiaman?"

"Oh, the Indiaman, I think. I should be over the nausea by then and—"

"Lizzy?"

"Well, it will be much more suitable for your son to be born at Pemberley, don't you think?"

THE END

CPSIA information can be obtained
at www.ICGtesting.com
Printed in the USA
BVOW03s0430281117
500828BV00006B/99/P